MW01244303

GONE WITH THE GHOST

Murder by Design

ERIN MCCARTHY

Gone with the Ghost is a work of fiction. Names, places, and incidents either are products of the author's imagination or are used fictitiously. Any resemblance to actual events, locales, or persons, living or dead, is entirely coincidental.

Copyright © 2017 by Erin McCarthy

Cover art by LLewellen Designs

All rights reserved.

Connect with Erin:

Facebook

Goodreads

www.erinmccarthymysteries.com

New release info: Newsletter

Chapter One

THE DAY I tried to kiss my best friend Ryan he killed himself.

Seriously. I confessed my love after a decade of friendship, he scratched his head and said, "Whoa, didn't see that coming," then left my house and ate a bullet.

So six months later, when I stumbled into my kitchen (painted citrine-green to promote happy thoughts) at six a.m. and saw Ryan standing there, I did the only thing that seemed appropriate. I screamed. At the top of my black, former-smoker's lungs. I knew I wasn't dreaming. The coffee was perking on a timer just like it should be, and I had a full bladder and morning breath—all signs of reality. But that was Ryan standing there wearing a navy-blue T-shirt and jeans, looking very much alive and sporting a full grin. Yet Ryan was dead. Dead, dead, dead. Flat-lined, DOA, pushing daisies, In Loving Memory inscribed headstone *dead*.

I'd been to his funeral. I'd cried enough tears to float an SUV downriver, and had suffered so much guilt and anxiety I was on the edge of cracking. Snapping into a dozen powdery pieces like peanut brittle dropped on a hardwood floor.

Ryan winced. "Jesus, Bailey, turn it down. It's the crack of freaking dawn."

Hearing him speak startled me so bad I cut off mid-scream.

My jaw worked for a second before I managed to stutter, "R-R-Ryan?"

"In the flesh," he said, holding his arms out. Then he laughed. "Or something like that, anyway."

"You're dead," I said, which wasn't the most brilliant thing I've ever said, but I was feeling like I'd been clocked with a brick. My ears were ringing and my chest felt crushed, like it did whenever my mom's cat took a snooze on my breasts.

He leaned on the marble counter and crossed his feet, which were shod in his favorite hiking boots. The ones his mother had insisted they bury him in.

"No kidding. Where have you been, Captain Obvious?" Then he leaned a little closer to me, studying my face. "Do you have the flu or something? You look like hell. Not that I know what hell looks like, since I'm stuck in purgatory. And I'm so freaking bored, I might actually be willing to take a chance on hell. But anyway, you look wrecked."

"Uhhh…" I reached a tentative hand out, thinking to touch him, I guess.

"You can't touch me, Bailey." The smile wavered on his face. "I'm a ghost, though I don't really like that word. It's too dramatic for me."

My hand froze in mid-air. He was a ghost. *Ryan was a ghost.* How incredibly and totally bizarre. Heart racing to rival a hummingbird's, I reached for the phone.

"What are you doing?"

"I'm calling 9-1-1, because I'm having a heart attack."

"Hold off a minute on that, will you?" He ran his hand through his short brown hair. "I need to ask you some things…like how long has it been since I bit it? They won't let me have a calendar in purgatory. I mean, what kind of a rule is that? Why does it matter?"

"It's been six months." Six long, horrible months. Picking up the phone, I clutched it to my chest and stared at him in wonderment. I had always thought ghosts would be transparent, wispy sort of things, moaning or gazing in longing at the living. Ryan

2

looked like he always had. He looked alive, healthy, exactly as if nothing had happened at all.

"Six months? Are you serious? Man, I thought it was more like a month." Ryan glanced at his watch. "I'm going to have to keep an eye on that. Scary." He shook his head. "Are you dieting? I think you should stop. That emaciated look doesn't work on you. With your red hair, you look like an Irish orphan. You've got smudgy black circles under your eyes too, and it ain't mascara, babe. Why don't you fix yourself some eggs and bacon for breakfast?"

Maybe I really *was* sleeping and my stomach was sending messages to eat protein in the guise of a concerned Ryan. Very sneaky. Got to watch that tricky little piece of anatomy—you turn your back for a second and your stomach is completely in charge.

"I haven't been hungry." In fact, the thought of scrambled eggs made me gag behind my hand. I picked at my sleep T-shirt and went for the coffeepot. Some things can't be faced without caffeine, and the ghost of my best friend was one of them.

"You got any appointments today? Stop off at the Bob Evans first and get loaded up. Nothing like a little butter to put the color back in your face." He sniffed the air. "Man, I wish I could pick up a mug. I'm dying for a cup of coffee. That's purgatory humor, by the way. *Dying* for a cup of coffee."

Yeah, I was just cracking up.

"Umm, I have to stage a house on Avalon at ten, but I'm free until then. I was planning to catch up on some social media, clear out my email." I also was planning to measure Ryan's West Park ranch house, that his parents had finally put on the market, hiring my staging company, "Put it Where?" to get it ready for a quick sale. But it seemed rude to bring that up.

"Good. I don't know how much time I have to hang with you, so drink your coffee and let's plan our strategy for finding my killer."

It's embarrassing to admit, but at this point I completely lost it. Hysterics are not usually my forte, but I had spent the last six months *suffering*. We're talking sobbing myself to sleep, therapy, guilt hanging like a choker around my throat kind of six months.

And here he was, Mr. No Big Deal. Like strolling into my kitchen was expected and nothing out of the ordinary.

"Killer? Did you say *killer*? What are you talking about?" I said in something that could only be defined as a shriek, given that it rivaled an opera singer in pitch. "You killed yourself, Ryan, six months ago yesterday. You stuck your police department issued gun in your mouth and pulled the trigger in your car. You sent a text and you left a whole mess of people behind who *hate* that you're not with us anymore. It was selfish and shitty and it sucks and I miss you and I...I...just want you to know that."

My air gave out and I stopped to breathe.

"You think I killed myself?" Ryan stood straight up and stared at me. "Holy shit, how could you think that? I was murdered, Bailey, and I've come back so you can help me find out who my killer is."

"Oh," I said. It's not easy to be witty in these circumstances. If Ryan had been murdered, that changed everything. It altered the entire scope of my grief and shifted my guilt to anger and my shock to horror. "Can we have a do-over?"

His eyebrow went up as I gulped half a cup of coffee, hot liquid sloshing over the mug and onto my red shirt. I brushed frantically at my now wet chest.

"This is crazy, just absolutely bleepin' crazy! I want a do-over! I want to go back in time and erase February seventeenth. I want you not dead." My words crashed to a halt with a wheezing gasp. "Crap, I'm hyperventilating."

"Okay, take a deep breath, babe, come on now. I'd tell you to stick your head between your legs, but you're standing up and wearing no pants. I may be dead but I'm not in a coma, and that's more than I need to see."

"Wait." A horrible, humiliating thought occurred to me. "Do you remember coming over here the day you died?" And me trying to lay one on him. His quick cop maneuvers that allowed him to dodge it. The way he had stuck his feet back into his snowy boots at warp speed and muttered a few things at the floor that could have passed for a goodbye or a "Good God"—I was never sure which. Neither one was desirable.

If he remembered all of that, then *I* wanted to die.

"No, that's the whole problem. All I remember is c to your house. Then it's a blank until I pulled into the park. I don't even know what made me go to the park, a ᵤₙₜ know who was in the car with me. Because someone was. I know there was someone talking. Then nothing. I don't know what happened." He shook his head. "But I didn't kill myself, and I'm pissed that you would think I would. What the hell? You know me better than that."

"Ugh!" I gasped in indignation. How was I at fault here? "You sent a text to your mother! The department said you killed yourself, no question about it. Prints, powder burns, all that crime scene crap—they said it was clear that you did it. Going to see an old friend—me—is typical suicidal behavior. You transferred money, made a will, and drove yourself to a peaceful, private location that was meaningful to you!"

"The park was meaningful to me?"

He needed a sign that read Big Dumb Dead Man stuck to his forehead. Geez. "You told me you lost your virginity there!"

Understanding dawned on his face. "Oh. I'm with you now. Yeah, that's right, I told you about that, didn't I? Cami something-or-other. Can't remember her last name. She had a great…" His hands came up in front of him, then he cleared his throat. "Sense of humor. She was a fun girl. But I'd forgotten all about that park. Those were good times."

I rolled my eyes. "Your sensitivity is heartwarming." Then I remembered where my thoughts had been going. I know, a little slow on the uptake, but the dead rising at six a.m. tends to throw me off. "So you don't remember coming over here that day?"

"I said that already, Bailey. Keep up with me." Ryan started to pace, his hands in the pockets of his jeans.

He had no memory of my little moment of insanity. My pathetic little speech about how all the feelings I had for him were much more than friendship. That kiss. Ugh. That *attempted* kiss. I had nightmares about that moment, where my lips inflated into giant taco-sized suction cups attacking Ryan while he pointed his gun at me and told me to freeze.

Man, I was glad he didn't remember any of that.

Not that it really mattered, since he was *dead*, after all, but never underestimate the power of mortification.

"None of this makes sense."

No joke. Give the dead guy a gold star.

I watched him as he did another circuit back and forth in front of my French country cabinetry, marveling that I could smell him. The scent of fresh-cut grass clung to him, with an underlying hint of sport deodorant. Since Ryan had died in winter, but now smelled like summer, I wondered if the seasons changed in purgatory like they did here in Cleveland. It seemed like a possibility, because wouldn't purgatory replicate your real life? Or was it your own personal purgatory, like a Groundhog Day for eternity? Mine would be a slushy overcast day in March where everyone I know is in Florida on a beach and I'm stuck shoveling snow off my driveway with my power out. I banished the horrifying thought, worried if I lingered too long there, I would manifest it for my future afterlife.

"Why would the department rule my murder a suicide? I'm a detective, for God's sake. I worked with those guys. They should have thoroughly investigated my death. They should have known I wasn't suicidal."

"They were all at your funeral," I said, then realized immediately that wasn't helpful. It was like offering a band-aid to an amputee. Totally irrelevant at that point.

But Ryan rubbed his mouth and looked curious. "Yeah? How many people? Did they have the police bagpipe band? I always wanted the band to send me off."

"The band was there, and they played Amazing Grace on the pipes. Not a dry eye in the house. I guess if I had to estimate, there were at least five hundred people at the funeral. You got a nice plot at Holy Cross cemetery, by the way. Next to the fence, easy to find, but away from traffic."

The one thing I'm always aware of is the value of real estate, and his gravesite was premium because of its location, location, location.

I should know—I'd been there many times staring at his headstone, searching for answers, peace, and an understanding that didn't exist. Until maybe now. Murder was bad, but suicide was worse.

"Cool. My parents probably paid too much for it, but it's good to know I'm important to some people."

"You're important to me."

What? That wasn't a vow of love or anything. It was just telling the truth. It could be my only chance to say those words to Ryan before he vaporized in front of me or something.

"That's sweet, babe. You know you're important to me too. We've been friends a long time, and I'd do anything for you, and I know you'd do the same for me. That's why you have to help me now." He reached out and his hands rubbed my arms.

Only I didn't feel anything. They were touching me, but there was no sensation whatsoever. Only I could see him doing it. Hello. Freaky.

"This is very, very strange. Like the time I did acid in college and thought my roommate was a rabid dog wearing a figure skating costume."

"You dropped acid?" Ryan snorted. "That must have been hilarious. You going wild is like telling a nun to go party."

Well. Just because I was neat and tidy, and preferred to spend my weekends relaxing with a good, mind-improving (okay, I'm stretching here) book, suddenly I was a nun?

"There are sides to me you've never seen." I reached for my electronic cigarette, which I knew was a seriously bad habit, but when you're wound as tight as I am on a regular basis, you need something to dislodge stress.

I took a juvenile pleasure in taking a deep drag and blowing the scentless vapor cloud in Ryan's direction. This felt so normal, like old times. He hated my habit, and before I'd quit regular cigarettes he had been known to flush them down the toilet, break them in half, and run over whole packs with his unmarked cop car. I had weaned myself onto the vape two years earlier, then had quit altogether the year before. But Ryan's death had been a shock that had me reaching for my addictive comfort. Some people want the comfort of cheesecake, I wanted to suck down some cotton candy vapor.

"I thought you quit." He capped that statement off with a fake hacking cough. "As for you having secrets? Please. I've seen everything you've got."

He'd never seen me naked, but I didn't imagine he meant that. He meant I couldn't do anything that would surprise him. That he knew me too well. That I was safe and predictable and boring. In my second career, having left my post-college position as an evidence tech (I hate blood, so it was a lousy fit), I was a workaholic with a perky smile, neatnik habits, and zero social life.

My social life, or lack thereof, was his fault for making me fall in love with him, and ruining me for all other men. I used to be able to fake it. I could go for months and months without thinking about how much I'd rather be with Ryan. I would date and never worry that part of me knew I had stronger feelings for Ryan than I did for my latest boyfriend. That was when I was younger, and being propelled along by the excitement of sexual discovery.

Now I was twenty-eight, pretty sure I'd tried everything there was to do without getting too kinky, and no longer able to fight my feelings for Ryan.

So I'd told him.

And he'd killed himself.

Or not, said his ghost standing in front of me.

"So…you got sent back to solve your murder? I'll help you if I can, but my mind is concerned with things like square footage, not homicide. Remember how lousy an evidence tech I was?"

It had actually hurt our friendship when I had quit. Ryan had endorsed me with the department as a hard worker, but some of the crime scenes (actually, all of them) had not been my cup of tea. Plus I sucked at wearing sensible shoes.

"Did they give you any instructions or anything in purgatory?" I asked. "How long are you here for?"

I took another hit off my electronic cigarette. I was feeling a little better, getting the hang of this communicating with the dead thing. Ryan was just like he'd always been. Nothing was creepy or gross or disturbing. Okay, it was a little disturbing, but this was like cheating. This was allowing me the chance, the time, to say all the things I had spent six months wishing I could tell Ryan.

"They don't tell me shit up there. I found out I was killed, and I asked them for details, and they said they didn't know the specifics regarding my death. How is that possible? Like, if they don't know, who the hell does? So basically, I got pissed and told them to send me back and I'd figure it out on my own. They gave me permission if I agreed to follow some lame rules. Number one was that I can only be visible to one person, so I picked you."

Warm fuzzy feelings stole over me. "You picked me? That's so sweet! Even though I'm neurotic and vape and am not even remotely wild?"

He looked a little embarrassed, a hint of color in his cheeks. "Hey, we all have our flaws. And truthfully, I like you just the way you are. I guess opposites attract, even for friends. And I knew I could trust you not to freak out on me."

No freaking here. I was on it. I felt better for the first time since I'd gotten that devastating phone call six months earlier.

Ryan hadn't killed himself. He hadn't been horrified by my declaration of love (or if he was, he didn't remember it, which still worked for me). And out of all the people in the whole wide world, (five hundred mourners, you know), he had picked me to appear to.

"I figured you'd make up a little list and organize the hell out of an investigation."

Darn straight. I could muscle anything into a To-Do List. "Okay, we'll figure this out, not a problem. Let me get dressed real quick and you can give me the plan of attack. Tell me where to start."

I dumped my coffee in the sink, wiped the stainless steel with a sponge, thoroughly rinsed the mug, than deposited it in the dishwasher. I wiped the mouthpiece of my e cigarette and plugged it back into the wall charger. I never took it anywhere with me, because it was far too tempting to hold it between my fingers all day cigarillo-style and pretend I was looking sultry like Rita Hayworth, when really I looked like I felt guilty over using it, which I did.

"You need to take a look at the police report on my death. Who was the investigating officer?"

I had a vague memory of a rather smarmy dark-haired guy with an Italian name who hadn't been in the department when I'd worked there. I padded up the back stairs of my narrow Victorian house to the second floor. "I'm not sure. I'll be right back, I just need two seconds to change."

But when I walked into my bedroom, decorated in a mix of vintage and industrial pieces, heavy on the floral fabrics, Ryan was lounging on my bed on his side, head propped up by his hand.

"Hey, look what I can do," he said, clearly pleased with himself.

I stopped in my tracks and grabbed at my chest, scared witless. "Holy crap! Please don't do that again. I'm still alive, you know, and would like to stay that way. My heart can only take so much."

"Oh, come on, I have to have some kind of fun. Being dead is very boring. It's like sitting in the lab waiting for a blood test. Flipping through a gardening magazine with old people making phlegm noises in the back of their throat all around you."

"Now there's a disgusting visual, thank you for that." I headed into my walk-in closet. "Why don't you pop back out into the hall so I can get dressed?"

Instead, he appeared in the closet a foot behind me.

"Geez, quit it!" I dropped the hem of my T-shirt, which I had been hiking up past my hips, and scrambled away from him, tripping on the corner of a suitcase. "I would like a little privacy, please."

"Just get dressed, who cares? I want to hear about the detective on my case before I get called back to hell—I mean, purgatory."

I was not wearing a bra. I cared. "Close your eyes."

"Oh give me a break." But he shut them and leaned against a row of empty wooden hangers, which were waiting for my dry cleaning to be picked up and assimilated back into the closet.

I have a very organized closet. It gives me pleasure to see all the boxes of shoes, with photos of each pair attached to the front, lined up by color. Sweaters zipped into soft cases, handbags on hooks, and belts creating a colorful rectangle in the corner. Neat and tidy.

But it was weird that he was leaning and nothing was moving. "Hey, how come you can lean on things, but you can't touch me or pick up a mug?"

"I have no idea. Like I said, they don't tell me anything. I've spent the whole time since I died trying to get some information and all I get is cryptic non-answers. I'm a cop. I know BS when I hear it, and these guys have been handing me a load. They have to know what happened to me."

"Maybe they know, but they want you to figure it out. Maybe it's a test or something." I took off my T-shirt and put on a bra in less than two seconds flat. I immediately felt better once the girls were secure. Left loose in Ryan's presence, who knew what they might do. "Maybe that's why you're in purgatory instead of heaven. Or were you supposed to go to the light but you didn't?"

"There was no light anywhere. Trust me, babe. And I definitely feel like I'm in a holding pattern. So maybe you're right. Maybe once I solve the question of my death, I can move on."

The thought made me feel a little sad. Of course I didn't want Ryan hanging out in eternity's version of a waiting room, but on the other hand, I was getting extra time with him. I reached for a sleeveless, floral print shirt, hanging in the tops/business casual section of the closet.

"You really have lost too much weight."

"What?" I spun around and found Ryan staring at me critically. So much for his closed eyes. The aqua and yellow shirt was in my hand. Not on my body. Which meant I was only in panties and a bra, and he was staring at me. Damn.

"You look too skinny. Men like women with something they can grab onto."

Nice to know even in death he found me unattractive. I rolled my eyes at the hangers. "Thank you. I'll remember that next time I'm looking for a man to grab me."

"Hey, I just had a thought. I wonder if I can still get a hard-on?"

Good grief. "You could have kept that thought to yourself."

"No, I'm serious." Ryan sounded agitated, but I refused to look at him. "Man, I don't know which would be worse—never getting it up again, or getting it up and not being able to do anything about it."

We were wading into waters I could very easily drown in. "I'm sure there's a hot ghost or two in purgatory you can investigate this issue with."

"I can't wait that long—this is scary. Quick, just turn around and take your bra off. Let's see what happens. I have to know."

Nothing could get me into my shirt and wide-leg trousers faster than that. "You're not going to be aroused by me. We're friends. It's not the same." *Unfortunately.* "So forget it. I'm not taking my bra off in front of you. Pop into the Crazy Horse Saloon tonight and get the answers to all your sexual questions. That's what sixteen-year-old boys do."

I smoothed my shirt in place, finished buttoning my white pants and turned to face him. "Look, I'll help you do whatever it takes to find your killer, but I have to draw the line somewhere."

"I'd take my pants off if you asked me to."

It was tempting, but I controlled myself.

He bit at his fingernail, a clear sign he was stressed.

I sighed. The hard-on mystery was not going to be solved by me, but I could apply myself to the murder question. "The detective who called me had an Italian name. He was kind of, I don't know, overly nice. Oily, almost. He took a little too much glee in telling me that you'd, and I quote, "blown your brains out.""

That effectively distracted Ryan from his potential penis problem. "DeAngelo. That sounds just like him. He's thorough, a good detective, but borderline weird. Sometimes I wonder if he can solve so many crimes because his mind is just a little too close to a criminal's. Like a Dexter complex."

No one could ever accuse me of that. I'd hated when there was blood spatter at scenes I was fingerprinting. But DeAngelo? It was possible he was into it. "I think that would be an accurate description of the guy I talked to on the phone. He approached me at your wake and gave me more details than I wanted to hear." I was pretty sure that conversation was what had ruined my appetite permanently. "And when I was on the verge of vomiting, he asked me out."

"He asked you out at my *wake*?" Ryan looked horrified, which was a good approximation of how I had felt.

"Yes. He did."

"Mother-effer." He stood straight, his hands curling into fists. "Who does that? I always thought he was a little off, but we got along. Yet I'm not even in the ground and he's poaching on what's mine?"

Hold it. Do not pass go, stop right there, wait a manic minute. Everything about that statement was so right, yet so wrong. It was like winning the lottery, but doled out at a dollar a day. "What do you mean, *yours*? I'm not your wife, not your girlfriend, not even your ex. I am your friend. While I admit the timing was tacky and inappropriate, there was no reason what's-his-name couldn't ask me out. And no reason I couldn't say yes if I wanted to."

Which would only have happened if I'd taken a blow to the head and suddenly found short, smarmy, arrogant men attractive, but the point was, the choice was mine.

"Don't get your panties in a bunch. I'm just saying."

I wanted for the rest of the sentence, but none seemed to be forthcoming.

"So what do you want me to do, Ryan? Find the police report. Okay. Anything else?"

"Try to remember what DeAngelo told you. And call Marner —he should be able to get you the report and answer any questions you might have."

Marner was his former partner and good friend—his first name was Jake, though everyone but God and his mother seemed to have forgotten that. "Got it. I can do that."

Ryan patted the pocket of his jeans. "Damn, I have to go. They're calling me."

"You have a cellphone?" I asked in horror. That was my vision of hell—a phone ringing at all hours in my afterlife. Non-stop notifications.

"It's on vibrate." He pulled it out and glanced at it. "Text message. What? They're saying I didn't fill out my Request for

Reentry paperwork correctly, and I need to re-file. This red tape is killing me." A grin split his face. "Killing me, get it?"

"I'm glad to see you're taking this dying thing so well, and that you haven't lost your sense of humor."

"Got to roll with the punches, babe. And it's not so bad, just different. I'll be back as soon as I can."

Sudden fear gripped me. "Wait, Ryan, don't go—"

But he flipped me a wave. "Love you more than beer, Bailey. See ya."

And he was gone. Not like a puff of smoke or sugar dissolving in iced tea, but just there one minute and gone the next.

I needed another cup of coffee.

Chapter Two

"HI, I'M BAILEY Burke. Your real estate agent Allison Loren sent me."

"Christy Jenkins," said the woman who had the life I wanted. In her mid-thirties, she was gorgeous—firm body, everything still perky, makeup on point, eyebrows pure perfection. She had a hottie financier husband, two Mensa-worthy offspring, and a ninety-year-old Tudor mini-mansion with views of the lake. That she was selling because it was too small.

Five thousand square feet didn't really cut it for me either, but I'd be willing to suffer with it.

This was the only downside to my job.

Raging real estate jealousy.

Yet the flipside was I got to peek into tons of houses I would never have seen otherwise, and one of the many things I really loved about Cleveland was the architecture. The Jensen's neighborhood was a hotbed of Tudors built lakeside in the 1920s, and the details in those houses were always amazing.

"This is my husband, Tim," she said as I followed her into the foyer. Tim gave me a wave and a smile before retreating to the back of the house, his phone in hand.

"You have a lovely home," I said. The challenge of having high-end clients was they tended to push back when I suggested changes. Yet, if anything, they needed staging more than a starter home client, because their buyer pool was both small and finicky. Everything had to be perfect for every single showing.

"Thank you. How should we do this?"

"Let's have you go through the house with me. I'll make suggestions based on my immediate impressions, then I'll send you a more detailed list with 3D images of the rooms with my changes implemented."

Tablet in hand to take pictures and measurements, I braced myself to find the correct wording to not offend her or make her think the opposite—that my services weren't even necessary.

But I have to admit, I wasn't as inclined as usual to feel green, even as I walked into a mahogany-paneled library filled with enough books to keep me busy for the next three thousand weekends. I was too distracted with thoughts of Ryan.

Wondering if I had lost it and it was all a figment of my imagination. Hoping I wasn't insane and his ghost was real, as much as a ghost can be. Wishing he would come back. Thinking there was no way in hell little old Bailey Burke could solve a murder. I couldn't even solve the mystery of where my newspaper went every morning. Sometime between delivery at 5a.m. and my opening the front door at 6:30 it habitually disappeared, and I had no suspects. Though I had my eye on the old guy across the street, because I had seen him reading a newspaper, and most likely, we were the only two people on the entire west side still doing that.

But this was murder. What did I know about murder? The closest I came was the rage that blanketed me when the neighbor's Rottweiler left brown bombs the size of a small child in my tiny front yard. Normally, I lived a very conflict-free life. I squirm when people say mean things to each other. I had retreated into the world of pretty things and design after my debacle of a stint as an evidence tech.

As we investigated the living room and formal dining room, I made notes but told Christy, "So far the only clutter I'm seeing is in your husband's office." It was littered with papers and laundry and something that may or may not have been an actual human skull. There was also a glass gun cabinet filled with a dozen rifles and the walls were lined with taxidermy out the wazoo.

"Stay out of my office," Tim called, his head popping into the hallway, startling me. He had a booming, insurance salesman voice at complete odds with his lean build.

I looked at Christy for a cue on how to handle that statement.

"Don't be stubborn," she told him. "You said we need to sell the house, Timmy. It was your idea. Did you see the new listing I sent you?"

"It's fifty grand overpriced," Tim said. "And did you see the roof? What the hell is that?"

"It's slate," Christy protested. "It's original. The owners have it checked and repaired every year. It would cost more than fifty thousand dollars, easy, to have a roof like that put on today. It has great resale value."

"It looks old," he said in disdain.

Um, because it *was*? That seemed to be the appeal of original for most people.

"I'm happy to leave your office alone if that's what you prefer," I told him. "Though I suggest you lock up your personal papers and any electronics that are easily removable, like your tablet and laptop. And you might want to lose the skull." Anything deceased tended to turn off potential buyers. General rule of thumb. "And make sure the gun cabinet is locked."

He gave me a nod, but he seemed more interested in the house his wife wanted to buy, that he was determined to hate. Tim shoved his phone at Christy. "Did you see this? That masonry needs repairs."

My thoughts started to wander as they discussed their housing future. I didn't care about the integrity of ninety-year-old brick at the moment. I cared about Ryan, who would never see forty, let alone ninety years on earth.

"Okay, sweetheart," she said, voice mild and unconcerned. "We can talk about that later. Bailey and I need to go through the house. I'm sure she has other appointments."

A date with the dead. That's what I had going on.

"Do you believe in ghosts?" I blurted to Christy after Tim

made a face and disappeared again. I was clutching my iPad with white knuckles like it was the only thing anchoring me to the floor.

She was startled by my random question, turning her gaze from the view of the lake through the six panel windows to me. Christy was about ten years younger than her husband, and about five years older than me. She had straight blonde hair, bouncy breasts and long, tanned legs that rose above her designer stilettos. Overall she gave the impression of perfection. Intelligent, sweet, and absolutely capable of getting what she wanted. With the kind of body men like to grab onto.

I vowed to eat a whole chicken for lunch to gain some protein.

She was also a woman who was bound to think I was certifiable for asking her something like that. It seemed more likely her hobby was golf or pilates or wine tasting, not ghost hunting. I was going to lose this job and future commissions from friends she might recommend me to because I was fixating on Ryan. Yet I couldn't stop myself.

But she nodded, apparently unperturbed. "Of course I believe in ghosts. Why do you ask?" she said, in such a normal conversational voice that I found myself reassured.

"Well. My dead best friend visited me today," I said, leaning a little closer to her, eager for comfort. "And I'm not sure how I feel about that."

Now okay, I admit that wasn't highly professional of me, but damn it, I had to tell someone. It was either that or sling back a pitcher of margaritas, and I've never been much of a drinker. I tend to wind up sobbing while listening to Sinatra on replay when I've had too many. Frank does it to me every time.

Ryan always thought that was funny. He would tell me I was only person who could find a song with the word "tramp" in it sentimental. My eyes started to fill with tears. Ryan was dead. Still dead.

Christy patted my arm, her mouth rounding in sympathy. "Oh my, well, that's sad but wonderful at the same time, isn't it?"

"Exactly!" I nodded enthusiastically. Christy understood.

"You want to see her, but at the same time, you want to know that she's found peace in the afterlife. And seeing her reminds you that she really is dead and won't ever be a true part of your life again."

"That's so true." Christy was clarity in cashmere. "Only she's a he."

"Ooooohhh." She squeezed my hand in sympathy, her cleavage Jiffy-Popping out of her sleeveless summer-red sweater. "*That* kind of friend. Just enjoy it, Bailey. Think of it as extra time with him. Not everybody gets that chance. And remember that you'll always keep him in your heart."

I blinked back the tears. "You're right, you're exactly right. Thanks so much, Christy." For telling me exactly what I wanted to hear.

"What's his name? Did he die violently? He may need help finding his way to the light." Now she seemed really interested, a spark of morbid curiosity in her eyes mingling with the sympathy.

"His name's Ryan, and he claims there's no light in sight. But then, he's a cop, a detective actually, and he tends to think he knows everything."

"Did he die on duty?"

I shook my head, not wanting to explain further. "He was shot."

Her eyes grew wide, so that I could see the rims of her green contact lenses floating over her pupils. "I remember that from the news. He killed himself, didn't he?"

Again, I couldn't do more than shake my head, shrug, and then give a half nod.

"Well then, no wonder he can't cross over. He's tormented over taking his own life. You need to reassure him. Release him from his guilt."

She looked so earnest, so worried, so solemn, I felt the need to reassure her, not Ryan. "Okay, Christy, I'll try. Thanks."

As we moved into the spacious kitchen, Tim was eating a sandwich standing over the sink. "Is she telling you that you need to scale back on your wine collection? Because she should."

At least I was right about the wine tasting hobby. Christy was a woman of layers, clearly.

"No, sweetheart, we're talking about ghosts." Christy shot him a dimpled smile, the tragedy of Ryan's tortured soul quickly forgotten as she flirted with her husband, wrapping her arms around his neck.

He rolled his eyes and turned his head to finish chewing. But he then smiled indulgently at her and I wasn't just jealous of their real estate. I was jealous of that—a man looking at a woman with love and affection. I needed to get out there more, clearly.

I tried to discreetly blow my nose and stuff the wadded tissue back in my purse. Used tissues should just evaporate. The minute you crumple it into a little ball, disintegration should spontaneously occur so you don't find yourself with a handbag full of hard tissue balls with lint, dirt, and gum wrappers clinging to them. Too many tears today had made me stuffy.

"Nobody wants to hear your theories about ghosts, babe." Tim gave Christy's butt a quick pat before he set her aside. "And please don't tell me this house is haunted, because you know I think that's crap."

"Oh, but it is," she said, her eyes wide and innocent. She looked like an angel with double D's. Most men's idea of heaven, Ryan's included.

"I can feel it," she added. "That's why I'm finally agreeing that we need to sell this house that I love so much."

Ah, so that was the real story. Christy didn't want to move. Tim did.

He snorted, and polished off the last bite of his sandwich. "This house isn't haunted. Don't tell people that. And we are moving, Christy. End of story. I need more space."

Christy sashayed away from him on her heels. I could practically hear the stripper music booming with each dink-dink of her curvy hips. Her husband's eyes followed her movements.

She grinned at me when we were down the hallway and walked into a first floor guest suite. "We're not moving, trust me. I adore this house. It has soul. But I have to let Tim think it was his idea to stay. Men are a pain that way."

"I admire your confidence," I told her truthfully. "I can't get men to do anything I want."

"Just play up your assets," she assured me.

When I figured out what they were, I would jump on that. "I think you have more natural assets than I do." I gestured to my chest.

"Natural? *Hardly*. And I didn't buy the only pair." She grinned. "Just remember the three H's. Heels, hand jobs, heart. Wear the first, offer the second and the third, and he's yours."

Interesting life philosophy. I had done one and three with Ryan, but I wasn't touching the second. Literally. Even if I wanted to, I couldn't. That whole "bodiless entity" thing wouldn't allow it. "I'll keep that in mind. Now let's look in your coat closet and see if we can reduce the number of out-of-season coats you're storing in there."

But as I stared at a sea of furs, bomber jackets, dress coats, and puffers, all I could see was Ryan's mother dressed all in black, bundled up in a long winter coat, weeping on her husband's shoulder at Ryan's funeral.

She had asked me why he would commit suicide and I had said I wished we could ask him. They always say when someone is murdered the killer won't talk and the victim can't. But in this case the dead man *was* speaking and I needed answers that I wasn't going to find staging a stately home.

Time to get my Nancy Drew on.

The police station is not my least favorite place on earth—that would be the outhouse at my cousin Sara's farm—but it's pretty damn close.

The building downtown needed an extreme home makeover. Or a bulldozer mowing it down. Everything is dingy gray, a bit rancid, just a little sticky—sort of like the bottom of my shoes after going to the county fair.

I understand that corralling prisoners is not about aesthetics, it's about the safety of the officers and staff. But can't you be safe with sunshine-yellow walls? And there's no crime in having a few houseplants to perk the place up. If the accused is properly hand-cuffed, he can't pick up a spider plant and wing it at anyone.

I didn't think it would be wise to point this out though, since I was there to ask a favor, and during my days working at the station, I had complained to the point an unknown person had posted a printout that said "Glamour Cube" on the exterior wall of my cubicle and put crime scene photos all around it. It wasn't funny, but I had deserved it, to be honest. It's not a place for pretty.

Ryan's old friend Marner met me at the glass window and had the guard buzz me in. Ryan had become close friends with Marner when they both joined the force, when I was still in college getting the degree in criminal justice I'd done nothing with after my evidence tech tenure (and yes, my parents are still annoyed about that). I knew Marner by default, since I had been friends with Ryan first, and occasionally the three of us did things together. During my lame attempt at working crime scenes after Ryan had thoroughly lost patience with me, it was Marner who had constantly offered me reassurance and encouragement. He was a good guy. Easy to be around.

Once we all had even gone to Niagara Falls together, which sadly was the closest I've ever gotten to a wild weekend with two guys. I had slept in a king-size bed sandwiched between two men after the hotel messed up our reservation but the wettest I got the whole trip was on the Maid of the Mist boat ride.

It was with that depressing thought that I smiled at Marner.

"Hey, Bailey, how are ya? Long time, no see." Marner enveloped me in a hug, which startled me. He'd never hugged me before, except once at Ryan's funeral, and now he was gripping me hard, right in front of half a dozen detectives in their cubicles.

"I'm okay, Marner, how about yourself?" I tried to subtly extract myself. He had a hell of a grip and was wearing way too much aftershave.

"Hanging in there." He shrugged, but still didn't let me go.

"Good." I patted his back awkwardly, realizing that seeing me must bring up thoughts of Ryan. And Marner still thought Ryan had killed himself. He hadn't been granted the relief that I felt, and I wondered if I was allowed to tell him. I'd check with Ryan first, but it seemed like Marner had a right to know.

Finally he released me, but kept my hands tightly in his. "What brings you by?"

Weirded out that we were essentially holding hands, I kept my voice low. "Do you have a minute? Can we talk somewhere private?" I wasn't sure if what I was going to ask was exactly legal in the strictest sense of the word, so I didn't want a bunch of nosy-nelly cops listening in on our conversation. I couldn't say about other stations, but here this particular group of cops eavesdropped and gossiped like a group of grandmas. Replace the knitting needles with guns and they were one and the same, male and female detectives alike.

Marner is more serious than Ryan ever was. He has an intensity in his brown eyes that shows he's thinking, planning, processing. Ryan was always more impulsive, going with his gut. I like both of them. But I do love Ryan, and I think it's because he isn't like me at all. Marner and I can get a little solemn when left on our own together.

He studied me for a long second, than glanced up at the clock on the wall. "Sure, Bailey. Let me grab my wallet and we'll go to lunch. You want Italian?"

Wallet most likely meant his weapon. Marner always locked his gun in his desk drawer when he was at the office. I followed him back through the maze of cubicles and got a couple of waves and "What's up?" from men and women I knew, plus the very predictable "Yo, Bailey, how's that Irish Cream?"

This was a longstanding joke they all found hilarious and I realized I hadn't missed working here at all. As if there was any doubt. This time it was a familiar face—Detective Cox, who once upon a time I had made the mistake of encouraging because I had been young, he was gorgeous, and it had been flattering. Before I'd realized he was married.

"No," I told Detective Cox flatly. He was wearing a grin on his long face.

"How's the Put It Where? business?" he asked, leaning back in his chair. "I have a couple ideas of where to put it."

Sometimes you have what you think is a tremendously clever name for a business. I had thought that, truly. Only I had genuinely underestimated the number of grown men with adolescent humor. It wasn't the first time I had gotten remarks about "where to put it". Cox's comment brought muffled laughter from the guy to his left, who I didn't know. He must be a new hire. I also saw DeAngelo, the cop who had questioned me about Ryan, a few desks over. He was watching me. When we made eye contact, he waved.

Sexual harassment when I didn't even work there anymore was truly crap. I thought it was time to put an end to it.

"Knock it off," Marner told him. "You're being a dick."

I appreciated the intervention but I wanted to get the point across myself so I smiled and leaned closer to him. I opened my eyes wide, a la Christy with her husband Tim, and said, "Where would you put it? Do you want me to call your wife and tell her where you'd like to put it?"

It was enough of a break from my normal thinly veiled disgust that it seemed to confuse him. He swiveled his chair around so he was facing his desk. "That's okay."

That made me feel just a little bit smug. Bailey 1, Cox 0.

"Just ignore him," Marner said as he bent over his desk, fishing his keys out of his pocket. "He's an ass."

"He started it. What's this?" I pointed to a hand-drawn cartoon pinned to his wall. It was a stick figure lying on the ground in front of a car, yelling "Help!"

"I hit a bum by accident and this is the guys' idea of humor." He slid his gun into his holster beneath his suit jacket. Marner wore his suit well, very tailored and trim, and decent quality.

But he apparently mowed down bums. "You hit someone? Did he die?" I was a little horrified.

"Nah. Not a scratch on him. He was so drunk he walked right in front of my damn car."

Ten minutes later, we were staring at each other across the table at an Italian restaurant on the end of what was an up-and-coming neighborhood. This place had been in existence for sixty years and stood by the philosophy that good comfort food would always trump trendy decor. Scooting the faux grapes and ivy floral arrangement out of the center of the table, I tried to smile at Marner. It was a struggle, because he was looking serious again.

"I'm sorry I haven't called you," he said. "I should have. I should have checked to see how you were doing."

My throat closed. Guilt sat heavy in my stomach. I wasn't the only one grieving, yet I had been selfish, caught up in my loneliness. "That's okay. It goes both ways, you know. I haven't called you either."

"You've lost weight. Your clothes don't fit right."

Got it. I looked lousy. Thank you. I pulled my electronic cigarette out of my purse. Okay, so I had brought it. This was emotional DEFCON 1. I needed my security blanket. As I raised it to my mouth, Marner grimaced.

"You still smoking? Those things will kill you. You should quit."

"This isn't real smoking. I quit actual cigarettes two years ago."

"You still can't do that in here."

"Fine." But before I put it away I took a quick hit. That first drag is like a thorough kiss—smooth and satisfying. I know it's bad for me, but so is pollution, and I had quit smoking once already. I was like in phase two of quitting. No one seemed willing to give me credit for that.

The short, paunchy waiter came over and Marner ordered a bottle of red wine. Not a glass, but a bottle. "Aren't you on duty? Isn't drinking off limits?"

"I can have a glass. They'll re-cork it and I can take it home. You'll have a glass too, right?"

"Sure."

"And when I said you'd lost weight, I wasn't saying you looked bad. Not at all. It was just an observation. I was wondering if you'd lost weight because of Ryan."

There it was. His name was out in the open between us finally, and it hung there, like the vapor cloud from my electronic cigarette.

"Yeah, I've lost weight. No, it wasn't intentional. I haven't been hungry." I leaned back in my wrought iron chair, the legs wobbling on the tile floor. "I can't let it go, Marner, that's why I needed to see you. I don't think Ryan killed himself." That was as close to the truth as I was willing to skirt at the moment.

He didn't say anything for a second. Hand scraping across his angular jaw, he watched me. "Bailey…" he said finally. "Why does it matter? Ryan is dead. As much as we hate it, that's the way it is."

That surprised me, I have to say. Of all the things I'd expected him to say, dead is dead wasn't one of them. "Of course it matters! And I know we can't bring him back, but wouldn't it be better to know he didn't do it on purpose?"

"Would it?" He shook his head, dark eyebrows furrowing. "If I found out he was killed, I'd feel just as lousy, but in a different way. I'd be mad at myself for not helping him, just like I'm mad at myself for not knowing he was unhappy. Either way, I let him down as a friend, and either way he's still dead."

Tears rose in my eyes before I could stop them. "Marner." Now it was me reaching for him, wanting to give him some kind of comfort. "Neither one of us could have done anything, either way. But don't you think Ryan's mother would rather know he was murdered than that he killed himself? And Ryan wasn't suicidal. *You* know that. *I* know that. He's the most happy-go-lucky guy I know. Knew."

Damn, I hate the whole past tense thing when someone dies. Needing to lighten the mood (or emotionally hide, you be the judge) I joked, "If *I* haven't killed myself, than surely Ryan wouldn't."

Marner jerked in his chair, horror on his face. "You're not considering that, are you?"

"No!" I yanked my napkin off the table and spread it across my lap. "Geez, I was kidding. Going for a laugh to ease the tension."

"Shit." He poured two glasses of wine, handed me one, and inhaled the other. Slapping the glass back on the table, he ran his hand through his short dark hair. "Don't say stuff like that, not even joking. It's not freaking funny."

It wasn't. He was right. Feeling guilty and embarrassed, I

drained half the wine to avoid saying anything for a second. My cheeks felt slapped, and my limbs numb, like the air conditioning was up too high. Forcing my mouth open, I managed, "I'm sorry, I didn't mean to upset you."

"I care about you, you know."

For a guy who normally never speaks unless spoken to, and who is more comfortable with electronics than women, this was a huge deal. The tears I'd been wrestling with all day shot out like a fire hose on high.

"I...I...care about you too," I managed to say before dissolving into high volume sobs.

People at the tables surrounding us were gawking, but I couldn't stop myself. It was so damn sweet. I hadn't bothered to call Marner in six whole flipping months, and still he cared about me.

Marner got that panicked man look and said, "Hey, hey, now, it's okay. We're cool. And if you want me to look into Ryan's suicide, I can do that."

I nodded, blinded by tears and struck by inspiration. "And can you get the police report for me to look at? I just need some closure, I think."

"Sure, sure. Have some more wine." He filled my glass to the rim.

What? It's called taking advantage of an opportunity. I wasn't *trying* to play Marner or be manipulative. The tears were real. But if they worked in my favor, all the better. If I was going to humiliate myself in public, there should at least be some benefit to it.

I wiped my eyes, gave a shuddery sigh, and drained my second glass of wine. Or was it my third?

Which is how I wound up drunk at Ryan's ranch house.

Chapter Three

CONSIDERING MY LEGS felt like they might slide out from under me at any given second, I decided to give up on creating a staging plan and started picking through Ryan's remaining belongings instead. Unfortunately I hadn't realized the real estate agent was showing the house ahead of officially listing it, and I walked in on her touring the house with clients.

I should have abandoned the entire project since I had pulled out of the station, clipped a bush and the curb, and promptly U-turned right back into the parking lot. I ordered an Uber, hugging my Coach purse to my chest and reciting the alphabet forward and backward. *A-B-C, what the frick is the matter with me? Z-Y-X, what stupid thing can I do next?*

I don't drink. Two glasses of wine was the equivalent of a gallon in my system. Not to mention that I hadn't eaten breakfast and had only managed to choke down three bites of chicken at lunch before my throat rebelled. The pricey red Marner had ordered hit me like cheap wine in a box and sent me reeling.

Mind whirling at the thought of the police report from Marner I had in my purse, and sauced up on Chianti, I couldn't seem to stop myself from going to Ryan's. I needed to be there, in his space, when I read the report.

"Oh, I'm sorry! I didn't realize anyone was here. I'm Bailey Burke," I said, after walking in on a woman Ryan's parents' age and her clients. My mouth lost control midway between the second and third consonant. But hopefully they'd just think I had a lisp.

They were a young couple and they looked like they had embraced the concept of conserving water. I know that I am excessively hygienic, bordering on compulsive, but I have a thing about nails. Fingers and toes. I immediately homed in on them, and I could see this couple hadn't touched soap in a while.

Their presumably white T-shirts were gray, with big yellow sweat stains in the pits, and the woman's pale-pink flip-flops had black toe outlines. Untrimmed toenails curled into her flesh, and her fingernails bore the remnants of a manicure from last winter, Christmas red, with cuticles the thickness and width of an old growth forest tree trunk.

My stomach did another sick flip.

"We need a place for our hissing cockroaches," the guy said to his agent as I went about my business measuring the living room. "Does this house have a basement?"

"Absolutely. It's full size and partially finished."

Ryan had kept his weights down there, along with a rather impressive collection of beer cans, both empty and unopened.

Ryan hadn't exactly been a super housekeeper, but he had never been dirty. I had felt comfortable sitting down when he lived there. His furniture was still in place and it was only two years old, a rustic plaid, heavy on the oak accents. His parents had taken most of his personal belongings, but in some ways that only made it worse. It was obvious he was never coming back. The house felt lonely. Abandoned.

I was supposed to be looking at it objectively, as a home stager. Not as his best friend. As a friend, I saw him sitting on that very masculine couch giving me a smile. From a design standpoint, it was dated and crowded. Yet it was hard to even think about that when there were strangers invading Ryan's space.

I've been in hundreds of houses, and they all have a unique feeling, an aura, a sense of calm or fatigue or excitement. Ryan's house felt empty, and that was hard to swallow.

Or maybe it was the wine belch that snuck up on me that was hard to keep down.

But I didn't want the cockroach lovers to have Ryan's house.

He wasn't coming back, but nice people without insects should have it. Maybe people with children who would laugh and run around.

"What's the yard like? We like to have parties in the summer." The wife snuffled up something from the back of her throat and let it fly into the sink.

"Uh…" The real estate agent seemed flummoxed.

I personally have never in my adult life witnessed spit leave a woman's mouth, unless it's my own and I have a cold. My head did a sort of disco twirl and my stomach strained to keep the wine in place.

"The yard is rather small," the agent said.

"As long as there's a spare room for our boa. We like exotic animals," the man explained.

Which was probably why he was fond of his wife, who was currently digging her panties out from their burial in her crotch.

"You know, now that I understand your needs better, there's a different house I'd like to show you. Can we reschedule for tomorrow? I can set up a new appointment for something I think will be a perfect match for you."

I could have kissed the agent. She gave me a grimace and a shrug when they both turned. I realized she was actually friends with Ryan's mother. I'd seen her at the church festival.

I tripped over the carpet runner Ryan had laid down in front of the door to the backyard. With the grace of a geriatric elephant, I slammed into the wall. "Oops, that rug just grabbed my shoe," I said, giving a brittle, over loud laugh.

They just looked at me. The client scratched his head. "I'm kind of busy tomorrow. I thought we were just seeing this house. It's not bad, but it's overpriced and man, this furniture is just garbage. It's hard to visualize how our stuff would go in here."

For some reason, that made me irrationally angry. It was so violating to have them there in the first place, then to hear them criticize the price sent me into emotional overload. Good. Let them think it was overpriced. *Bye, bye, exotic pet people.*

"I know the sellers," the agent said. "They won't budge on the price. It was their son's house and they can't take a loss on it. Let's look at something that has a little more property."

They drifted toward the front door and the agent gave me a final smile. "Should I put the key back in the lock box?"

"Yes, thanks." The minute they crossed the threshold, I shut the door as fast as I could. Something was wrong with my balance. I let the wall hold me up so I didn't puddle into a heap on the ceramic tile that marked the two by two foyer.

Going over to my purse, I fished out the police report. I had to see what it said. *Angle of the body, blood spatter, weapon discharged once...* It was very clinical. Very nauseating. Now wasn't the time to read this. I crammed it back into my purse and went for the couch, but then decided I needed a cold surface to soothe my hot and clammy face.

I went down on my knees, then stomach, oozing into a jellyfish impersonation, legs and arms sprawled out.

"What are you doing?" a familiar voice asked.

My cheek nice and cool on the tile, I tried to lift my head, to no avail. It had become too heavy for my neck. Amazing how that could happen. "Ryan?"

"The one and only."

His voice sounded far away and I tried to look over my shoulder and locate him, but that made me dizzy. I clamped my eyes shut.

"Why are you on the floor, Bailey?"

"I'm just resting." My wrist started to hurt from lying on it. I shifted a little and discovered a black streak from shoe tread on the tile. With my index finger I rubbed it out, then realized that was stupid because my purse with my antibacterial squirt foam was on the other side of the room.

"Are you sick or have you lost it?"

"I think I might be drunk." I gave a little giggle because it really did seem extraordinarily funny. I was talking to my best dead friend and I was plastered off a measly two glasses of wine. Or was it three?

"*Drunk?*" He sounded thoroughly shocked. "Drunk on what?"

"Wine. Marner took me to lunch and got me drunk." Blame him. I wouldn't have touched the stuff without his bad influence.

Ryan snorted. "Nice. Did he at least give you the report before he got you smashed?"

"Yep. It's in my purse."

"Go get it."

"You go get it. I'm paralyzed." Talking was an effort. And the room was doing a fair approximation of a Tilt-A-Whirl.

Concerned about the cleanliness of the floor, I put my cheek on my arm.

And promptly fell asleep.

～

The problem with a dead best friend is that they can't help you when you pass out drunk on their floor. I woke up twenty minutes later according to my FitBit app, stomach churning and head pounding, the muscles in my back locked in a painful spasm.

"All right, sleeping beauty, time to get up." Ryan was pacing back and forth in front of me. "You only drink like once every three years and you pick today to get trashed? Unbelievable."

"I've had a challenging day," I said with as much dignity as I could muster from the floor. But I did feel refreshed. The buzz was gone and despite the mild headache, I felt normal. As normal as a woman can feel talking to her dead bestie.

"Well, I've had a challenging three hours waiting for you to wake up while I sat in my empty house. I figured something out. I can't appear anywhere that you aren't."

I felt a rather selfish pleasure wash over me at that, despite the frustrated tone of his voice. "It was twenty minutes. Don't be melodramatic."

"I'm stuck being a shadow man and you're sleeping off having a good old time saucing it up. Do you know how bored I've been?

33

I can't even read the damn report because I can't open your purse."

"Don't get pissy with me." I lifted up onto my elbows and did a head check. It was still there on my shoulders, which was promising. The room didn't spin and my gut only felt like the wave pool at Cedar Point. This was probably as good as it was going to get. "For your information, I was crying over you at lunch—about how much I miss you, as hard as that is to imagine—and Marner, being a guy and clueless what to do when a woman shows the slightest sign of distress, plied me with Chianti to plug the tears."

I sat completely up and pushed my hair back off my face. Ryan was biting his fingernail.

"I'm sorry, Ryan, I didn't mean to spend my afternoon on your foyer floor. I only had two glasses of wine. Or maybe it was three." Possibly four.

He sighed. "I'm sorry too. I know this whole thing is a lot to ask of you, but I need answers."

"I do too." I grabbed an end table and hauled my sorry butt up. "So let's find some answers."

On wobbly legs, I went to my purse, which I had set on the table in the dining area. It couldn't be called a dining *room* since it was really a corner of the living room. But its tile flooring and brass chandelier gave it the privilege of being titled a dining nook.

"Here's the report." I set it down on the table for Ryan to look at and went into the kitchen.

Pulling a glass out of the cabinet, I searched under the sink for a sponge and dishwashing liquid. I knew they were still there because Ryan's mother came over once a week or so and dusted and cleaned the house to keep it from falling into disrepair. I'd often thought how hellish a chore that must have been for her, cleaning a house her son was never coming back to.

Sponge in hand, I washed the dust out of the glass and swallowed the thick, hot bile that had taken up residence in my mouth. With a country blue dishtowel, I dried the glass, ran the tap to get the water cold, and filled it to the top.

After draining two full glasses, I felt completely back. The water was sloshing around in my gut, but the pounding in my head had stopped and I could practically hear my cells quivering in gratitude at the promise of rehydration.

"I need you to turn the page," Ryan said in a tight voice.

I went and turned it without saying a word. He didn't look happy. I could understand why. The report was from the scene and it was not only gruesome, it was short. No one seemed to have questioned that it could be anything but a suicide.

"Where's the rest of the file?" he asked a second later when he'd finished scanning the page.

"That's all Marner gave me. The report from the scene. He flat out refused to give me the autopsy report. And the rest he said is psychological stuff—interviews with people you worked with, tracing your movements from that day, and interviews with family and friends. But I have to tell you, they interviewed me and they only asked me three questions."

"What did they ask?"

"When was the last time I'd seen you."

Twelve noon, February seventeenth.

"What your mental state was like at that time."

Agitated from my confession (not that I had shared that little piece of info).

"If I knew anything you might be upset about."

Nothing that he'd kill himself for.

"What'd you tell them?"

"You left my house at noon and you were fine. And that you were the least suicidal person I know."

Ryan smiled at me over the table. A real Ryan smile, where his eyes crinkled at the corners and his mouth spread wide. "Thanks, Bailey."

"It's true. That's why I've been such a freaking mess. I just didn't, couldn't believe you would kill yourself." I hadn't been able to believe it. But everyone had convinced me it was possible, and well, it appeared he had, so I had been forced to accept it. "They said you were upset over getting passed over for detective and that you owed quite a bit for student loans."

"I wouldn't kill myself because I owed ten thousand bucks for community college. You know money isn't important to me."

I shrugged. "Everything can be made to fit the puzzle. I had no choice but to believe the experts."

He made a fist and punched my shoulder, only I didn't feel anything. "It's okay, gorgeous, we're going to figure this out. Here's what we've got so far." He pointed to the file. "I'm in the park, why. We don't know. I left your house at noon... Is that an exact time?"

I nodded. I'd glanced at the clock when he'd left to record the moment I had ruined our friendship forever. "I looked at the microwave clock as you headed out the garage door. It was 12:03."

Ryan glanced at the report again. "I was found by Mikaela Stevenson and Barry Morris, both twenty years old, high school friends, both students at Cleveland State. They live in Lakewood in a duplex." He shook his head. "Who names their kid Barry? God, I'd shoot myself." Then he laughed. "Shoot myself. Damn, I'm a riot."

He made a motion like he was hitting a drum for the punchline.

I rolled my eyes, which only made me dizzy. "Maybe you can start a stand-up act in purgatory."

"So Mikaela and Barry are jogging together and they stop because Barry needs to tie his shoe, according to this report. You know what that means."

Of course I did. Duh. "That his shoe was untied."

"Try again. Mikaela and Barry live together so they're clearly a couple. Technically they could just be friends, but they're jogging together, heading into a very secluded part of the park where there aren't any trails to speak of, just a whole lot of trees, and rough, uneven ground. They're not expecting any cars because it snowed the day before and the little observation parking lot should be empty, the drive unplowed."

I was thinking really hard, but didn't see where Ryan was trying to lead me. "So why did they go there if they weren't jogging?"

Now it was his turn to roll his eyes. "Get with it, Bailey. They were going to get it on, or at least have a little alone time make-out session. They probably really were jogging, but then Barry's turned on by the way the wind is ruffling Mikaela's hair, and with a wink and a nudge he has her over in the trees. Because while it's not unusual for friends to jog together, going off trail would be odd for a platonic relationship when it's February and freezing outside."

I could feel my jaw drop. Not because of Mikaela and Barry's alleged relationship, but because it made a whole lot of sense that they were not just out for a stroll, and it had all been so easy for Ryan to see. A to B to C, he had logically taken the scenario through to its natural conclusion, all while I was pondering shoelaces.

I had no idea if Barry got Mikaela hot on the trail, but I knew *I* was turned on.

Ryan's cop thoughts were damn sexy. I needed to start dating again. It had been far too long since I'd even considered making out, let alone taking a walk in the woods, if you know what I mean. Though in February? Hell no.

Banishing the sudden need for a jog, I cleared my throat. "Okay, so assuming anyone is insane enough to have sex, or even make out, in a snow bank in the dead of winter, they were off the jogging path for a reason. So why was your car there? Same reason?"

Ryan grinned. "Good question. But if I was, at least I was smart enough to have a car to do it in."

If he had gone straight from my confession of love to another woman's arms, I really didn't want to hear it.

"But I seriously doubt that's what I was doing, since I distinctly recall having a guy with me, and that's not my type."

He wanted me to ask what his type was, but I refused to go there.

"Or maybe it was a woman. Or maybe I was alone." He frowned. "I don't know. It's fuzzy."

"Okay. Then?"

"So almost immediately Mikaela and Barry realize they aren't going to get the privacy they were looking for, but before they can jog on past, they notice something. There's something all over the window of the car. They can't see into the car on the driver's side, but it looks like someone has thrown up or splashed something over it, according to Mikaela. So they knock on the door, and as they're knocking, and the person inside isn't moving, they slowly start to realize that what they're seeing is blood and brains."

My stomach lurched and it wasn't from the wine. "Ryan."

He tapped his thigh, not looking the least upset. Just serious. Thinking. "So Barry pukes his guts out in the snow, while the girl calls 9-1-1. First officer on the scene is at 3:17 p.m., Officer Rick Pannaconi. After determining the victim is deceased, he secures the scene, takes Mikaela and Barry's statements, let's them go. He doesn't realize right away that this is a cop until he runs the plates and they come back as mine. He calls homicide, tells them its my car, calls the coroner. Enter DeAngelo. Exit Pannaconi and the end of this very worthless report. Why does DeAngelo immediately assume suicide? I don't get it."

I swallowed, forced myself to speak. "There was a text. One to your mom."

"That part bothers me. That means someone was planning to kill me, or panicked and pulled out my phone and sent a text. What did the text say, by the way?"

"I don't know. They never told me, but from what DeAngelo said, it wasn't elaborate."

"So a suicide text, probably something like "I'm sorry." How could I have let myself get into a situation like that? I must have had my head up my ass that day. Jesus."

Fresh guilt swamped me. He had probably been distracted by me, wondering how to let me down easily. How to tell me to take my lips and go find another cop to throw myself at.

"If someone was in the car with you, wouldn't they have wound up covered in blood? And how would they leave without anyone seeing them? Footprints in the snow and stuff like that?"

"Good point, Bailey. But I'm guessing any footprints were wiped out by Mikaela and Barry, then Officer Pannaconi walking all around the car. Preserving a crime scene wasn't on their minds at that point. If all evidence at the scene pointed to suicide, they wouldn't have any reason to think homicide initially, though usually detectives make no initial judgment. They wait for facts. But any evidence they overlooked would be gone in a day. Drops of blood in the snow, footprints, all would have disappeared with the first melt or next snowfall. But I don't like the fact that they were so quick to rule it suicide. That's not like those guys. You know. You know how meticulously they pour over a scene."

Lowering myself into a dining room chair carefully, afraid of any residual head spinning, I scanned the report again. It seemed very cut and dried, clinical. The only revealing fact was that Officer Pannaconi couldn't spell worth a damn. He had a repeating consonant issue. Arrive was arive, pattern was patern, and officer was oficer. In reading it, I was tempted to put on a French accent.

I was starting to wonder if Ryan had it wrong. He didn't remember, after all. Maybe he did commit suicide. I didn't even know what to think at this point.

"Where is my car?" Ryan asked.

"I don't know." The truth was, I hadn't asked a lot of questions. The answers might have been something I didn't want to hear. My stomach rumbled.

"You hungry? I guess its dinnertime, isn't it? Why don't you order a pizza?"

Hunger might explain that burning feeling in my intestines, or it might be a lacerated ulcer. I was figuring the latter was probably closer to the truth. "I'm fine."

"No, come on. You need to eat. It'll be my treat."

"You have money?" I asked in amazement.

He frowned. "No. Guess not. Sorry. But you still need to eat something. Maybe there's food left in the kitchen."

Not likely. His mother was a very thorough housekeeper. She wouldn't leave Shredded Wheat around for six months, getting stale and attracting mice. "I'll just order a pizza. Though I sure in the heck can't eat a whole one all by myself."

Ryan lay on the couch, eyes closed, fingers pressed to his temples, in deep thought as I ordered a pizza. I argued with the pizza guy when he said I couldn't get just a personal pan pizza delivered. By the time it was hashed out to our mutual satisfaction (upgraded pan pizza to small, two toppings, with a 2-liter of Pepsi) Ryan had sat up straight, feet on the carpet, hands in his lap.

"Earlier you said they concluded it was suicide because of the texts, and because the park was meaningful to me. How did they found out about all of that shit? I never told anybody but you about Cami with the big chest in the park."

My sympathy for Cami grew. What is it about men and breasts? Freud had it completely backwards—I don't know a single woman who feels an ounce of penis envy, but every man I know wishes he could walk around all day playing with breasts. If they could squeeze a pair at random intervals whenever the urge struck maybe the world would be a less violent place.

Of course, I wasn't the least put out that Ryan was a breast man and I had none to speak of. It didn't matter. We were *Just Friends*, and he was dead, after all. But that didn't stop me from throwing my shoulders back and thrusting out a bit. Damn it. I didn't want to be like that.

"Why would DeAngelo notify you that I had been killed?"

Right. That was the important part of this discussion.

The timing was confusing me now, but after that first horrible conversation with DeAngelo, Marner had come to see me. "DeAngelo was the one who told me, and he didn't spare me any details. He's the one who asked the basic questions. I'm guessing it was because we had been texting that morning. He wanted answers, I guess. But then later that night, Marner stopped by. He's the one I told about Cami. I didn't know you made out a will. It was Marner who mentioned it when he was trying to explain that it was suicide." I squirmed at the memory. "I had sort of flipped out on him."

Lots of screaming and crying and pounding my fists against him. A real cliché. No wonder the guy had panicked and poured wine down my throat that afternoon—he must have been terrified he'd be dealing with a repeat performance. Not wanting to dwell on either embarrassing episode, I quickly asked, "Why did you make a will?"

His reaction wasn't what I expected. Ryan got sheepish. "There's a law office across from the department. There was this woman lawyer. I'd see her going in and out of her office. She was hot. I mean, *really* hot."

Oh, for the love of margaritas. I could see where this was going. "And?"

"I went over and made a will because I wanted to talk to her, maybe ask her out."

What did you want to bet she had curves. "Did you ask her out? I didn't know you were dating anyone."

He waved a hand in dismissal. "She already had a boyfriend. But I got a will made, which, as it turns out, was damn good timing."

I wasn't going to point out that my feelings had been just a wee bit hurt that he hadn't left me anything. I'd reassured myself that guys didn't think like that. They didn't leave their Gretzsky signed stick to their brother and their collection of beer cans to their cousin. They didn't leave behind love notes for their female best friend indicating how they returned her feelings, and they didn't have any jewelry to dole out.

At least not Ryan, anyway.

Everything had been left to his parents, with his modest insurance policy going for his funeral expenses and the remainder into a trust for his sister's kids to pay for their education.

Colleen had cried when she had told me that, when I had run into her at Ryan's house three months ago. She had been helping her mother clean up the yard, which had gone wild during the spring when no one had been able to bring themselves to tend to it. She had told me that while it was wonderful of Ryan to think of her girls, she'd give everything she had and then some to have her brother back.

Maybe I should tell him. "Colleen told me about the money for the girls... She said she'd give it all back and then some to have one day with you."

Which reminded me what a gift I had. I couldn't touch him, but I could talk to Ryan, and I needed to enjoy that.

Ryan shrugged. "It wasn't much, but those kids are smart and they should go to college. Hopefully it will help her and Jim out."

Apparently he wasn't in the mood to get sentimental. All righty. His mind was still working around the facts of the case. I could appreciate that. I was a workaholic myself.

"It sucks that I can't be in the station without you. Marner only gave you about a tenth of the file on me, I'm guessing. There aren't even any photos of the scene. We need to see those to get an idea of the direction the blood spatter and blowback went."

We didn't need to see any such thing. There was no way I wanted to take a looksie at pictures of Ryan with half his face blown off.

"I can ask Marner, but I doubt he'll give them to me." He was a little more protective, more traditional. Ryan was the kind of guy who figured "hey, you asked to see it", but Marner was more of a "you don't know what you're asking to see" kind of guy.

Maybe it was time for me to start listing the facts of the case as we knew them. Pulling out a pad of paper from my handbag, I gave it a header with my Bailey Burke, "Put it Where?" pen.

<u>Evidence of Suicide</u>
Will (actual result of lust, not depression)
Texts (what did they say?)
Location (coincidence?)
Lack of motive for murder?
Powder burns

When I wrote that Ryan stopped reading over my shoulder. "Hold it. Powder burns on what? My hands?"

"You tell me, Detective Conroy. But I distinctly recall DeAngelo talking about powder burns."

"You had a hell of a conversation with him, didn't you?" Ryan's blue eyes were curious, his nostrils flaring just a little.

"At the time, it seemed disgusting, macabre, and the punishment for all my earthly sins, but in hindsight, yes, it does come off as pretty odd."

"I think it's time for you to pay a little visit to DeAngelo."

Yuck. I pictured DeAngelo's smarmy grin and that tuft of chest hair that always burst above his top button. Double yuck. Seeing him twice in the same day seemed like cruel and unusual punishment. "I was afraid you were going to say that. I'm not even really drunk anymore, which is a shame. He's the kind of guy you need to see through wine goggles."

"I'd do it for you."

"I know." And I'd do anything for Ryan.

Except show him my breasts.

No sense in deflating both of us.

"Can I at least eat my pizza first? I'm sure after talking to DeAngelo my appetite will be gone."

Chapter Four

I GOT A reprieve. When I called the station, DeAngelo had left and wouldn't be back until the next day. Since there was no way in hell I was tracking him down at his cave, or house, or the rock he lived under, I was off the hook until morning.

"I can't believe you're going to waste all that pizza." Ryan stared at the box in front of me with longing.

"I'm not. I'm taking it home. I'll eat some more tomorrow." I had only managed to force down one piece. My inability to chew and swallow was starting to bother me. Maybe it was time for a physical. Maybe my weight loss wasn't grief, but some wasting disease or cancer or hepatitis.

That was a cheery thought.

"Are you coming with me?" I asked as I started turning off overhead lights, and flicking the stove light on so the house would look occupied. "I have to go get my car at the station, then I'm going home and straight to bed."

"How are you going to get your car?"

"I'm taking the bus." I could take an Uber again, but I felt the need to punish myself. It's a Catholic thing. We thrive on guilt.

"Shit. No thanks. I'll just zap myself over to your house once you're back. That's one of the few cool things about being dead."

"Can't you like, suck me over there with you? I don't want to take the bus either." Especially now that I had missed the rush hour crowd. Seven o'clock RTA riders were a little quirky.

"It doesn't work that way. And maybe I'll just catch up with you tomorrow—let you sleep tonight."

"How *does* it work?" I grumbled as I gathered up papers and stuck them back in my purse.

"I'm not really all that sure. I'm looking into it. But there are rules, you know, for when I'm among the living." He grinned. "Doesn't that sound asinine? Among The Living... I feel like an eighty-year-old church organist when I say that."

That's not what he looked like. He looked delicious. All cute and sexy and tousled. I sighed.

I clicked off the chandelier in the dining nook. With all the blinds closed it had been necessary for my list making. "Please tell me you're going to be there when I talk to DeAngelo tomorrow. I know what you want me to ask him, but what if he leads me in the wrong direction? Or worse, he gets creepy on me?"

We had made a list of questions during my pizza eating, but I had no trouble picturing myself choking during the interview and winding up the butt of jokes around the station. Wait. I already was. Great, nothing to lose then.

"It shouldn't be a problem. What day is tomorrow?"

"Wednesday."

"Okay, that's cool. I have a class at seven, but we'll be done long before then."

It took me a second. "A class? You have continuing ed in purgatory?"

"It's my Intro to Death course. The prof has it out for me and he'll bust my chops if I'm late."

Now that the lights were out I couldn't really see his face in the dusky room. "Are you serious?" He had to be joking.

"Yeah. He's tough."

Ryan *hated* school. I had met him my first day at community college. I was bustling to my psychology class, desperately eager, and he was ditching out on his criminal justice class. He'd tripped me "on accident", which he later admitted was on purpose, because he had wanted a distraction to justify missing class.

He'd scooped up my books, apologized profusely, and walked me to my class. Then met me for lunch. Halfway through my turkey on whole grain I was head over heels for him. His charm, his sense of humor, his impulsiveness and borderline recklessness had all appealed to me.

I'm not sure why he became friends with me, though I do think he originally had intentions of loosening me up. Pretty fast he found out not much loosens up a jar screwed as tightly shut as I am.

The idea of Ryan forced to sit through lectures in purgatory was downright hilarious. I laughed as I lifted the pizza box and wiped the table beneath it with a napkin.

"It's not funny."

"Yes, it is. If you need help studying for your exams, let me know. I make a good study buddy."

"You are a good buddy, Bailey." He gave me an earnest smile —or as earnest as Ryan gets anyway.

Now, after the whole back from the dead thing, the murder revelation, the tears, the wine, the random strangers tromping around his house, and the prospect of staring down DeAngelo, this is what nearly did me in. The way he looked at me, like he could swallow me whole, just suck me into his aura, the way a man looks at a woman, with *that* expression. You know the one. His eyes, how they twinkled, his nose…no, no, no, that's Santa.

I'm not sure what it was, but at that second, I felt that maybe, just maybe Ryan shared some of the feelings for me that I had for him. My body, led by my lips, started toward him for a brief second of insanity before I remembered he *didn't* feel that way about me. Not to mention that sticky issue of lacking a solid body with which to kiss.

"I'll always be your good buddy," I said in a soft voice.

The mood broke. He shook his head, laughed. "See you in the morning, you lush. And don't feel embarrassed about the snoring and drooling. That's normal for drunks, and I'm used to it."

Oh. My. God.

Ryan disappeared and I whimpered.

It seemed a fitting ending to the day.

~

Only the day wasn't over yet. On the bus, I got a call from Tim Jensen.

"Hello. This is Bailey Burke." Your emaciated and neurotic home stager.

"This is Tim Jensen. I wanted to let you know we're making an offer for a house on Lake Road."

So Christy had lost the battle to stay in her home. "That's fantastic, Tim. Congratulations." I paused and waited for him to explain why he was calling.

"Well, it wasn't really Christy's first choice, but I told her this one makes the most sense financially, and purchasing a home isn't about emotion."

I'm sure Christy felt put to rights about the whole thing after Tim had explained it to her. *Puh-lease.*

My annoyance increased when Tim continued. "I need you to get our house staged by the end of day tomorrow. We're going to go to a hotel with the kids and we need it listed by Friday."

"That's quite a time crunch." I'd have to consume a *vat* of wine to agree to do a three day job in eight hours. "I can get it done by Saturday morning, but I'm going to have to charge you an expedited fee." My mind started racing with furniture placement plans and how to wrest the clutter in his office away from Tim.

"Whatever it takes. We need the house sold in a week."

The man across from me bumped my leg with his foot and muttered an apology. The bus wasn't even crowded, why did he have to align himself directly across from me? And was he drooling? But hey, I'd seen myself in the mirror at Ryan's when I'd gone to evacuate the wine, and I looked like something the cat not only dragged in, but mauled, licked, tossed in the air, and finally swatted under the fridge. This guy appeared to have suffered a recent electrocution, so maybe we were magnetically drawn to each other.

Mutant bookends.

"Thanks for understanding. I'll be there at seven a.m. with my team." I was going to have to beg Alyssa and Jane to come in early. Alyssa was a good friend of mine and had been since high school, who had a full time night job in IT but who liked to work for me part-time to indulge her creative side. She would grumble but relent. Jane was twenty-one and more interested in her social media and how she was perceived on it than her job. But she was cheap and she worked on an as-needed basis. The business could only sustain me full-time. So far.

The bus reached the stop at the corner by the police station. As I got off the bus, I called Alyssa and explained the situation.

"That's fine," she said. "I'll stop and get us jumbo coffees and I'll meet you there."

"You're awesome. I owe you."

The parking lot was kind of creepy at night, with its apricot floodlights working weakly against the encroaching dark. Hustling, I unlocked my car via remote, taking a look at my less than superior parking job earlier. There was a solid three feet of empty space at the front of the spot and the left back bumper was hanging out in an arch, like I'd been completing the turn and just got too tired to finish.

Bad choices. I gave silent thanks that I hadn't driven that car more than three feet. If life ever called for a series of hashtags this moment was it. #lightweight #staysober #ghostswillmesswithyourhead.

"I want to collect on that this weekend. Promise me we can do something fun after this house is done, even if it's just shopping and a movie. You've been hiding out at home and it's not healthy," Alyssa informed me.

I grimaced. I had been. It was true. "That sounds fun. I'm in." We said our goodbyes.

Worried that a cop might pop out from around the hood and order me to take a breathalyzer, I got in and drove home, alert, straight-backed, and respectful of all traffic laws. I was not the least bit drunk any longer, obviously, but I was exhausted and horrified by my behavior, inadvertent or not.

I like rules. I live by order. It was a personal embarrassment that I had succumbed to anything resembling recklessness. But I'd been trying to ignore my emotions for six months, pretending I wasn't drowning, and you can't do that forever. It will drag you under and steal your breath at some point, and today wasn't a day to feel guilty about anything. Today was a day to appreciate the fact that I was still standing. I mean, after I'd peeled myself off the floor.

A shower was needed to restore my sense of equilibrium and cleanliness, and then I would call Jane and the furniture rental company. Then Bailey Burke was hitting the hay.

Except when I pulled onto my street, there was a car in my driveway. I live in a old neighborhood full of restored homes called Ohio City. The houses are mostly Victorian, and driveways are narrow, with parking at a premium. Squatting on someone else's sliver of concrete is totally taboo and a legitimate cause to call the cops if you don't recognize the vehicle. The trouble with trendy was every single lawyer and IT guy wanted to grab a drink at one of the neighborhood microbrewerys or speakeasy-themed bars, snagging every street spot for blocks.

I loved the vibe of the old houses though, and it was worth any inconvenience. Normally I would shrug it off and knock on the neighbor's house to see if they knew who the car belonged to. It was probably someone visiting my next-door neighbors who had pulled into the wrong side, since the driveways did actually touch. It wasn't technically a shared drive, but it could cause confusion.

There was no room to squish my perky SUV anywhere but behind the dark car, so I parked as close to the bumper as I could and got out. It was tempting to just leave it there and go in my front door without dealing with mystery car, but then I figured it would be my luck the person would tear out of my drive and nail my mini-SUV, not realizing I had parked there.

I was debating which neighbor's door to knock on when I saw there was a man sitting in the driver's seat of the car, and his door was opening. A shiver ran through me and I reached for my cell-phone. It was dark, and my mother put the fear of Freddy Krueger in me as a kid. Woman+dark+strange man=throat sliced.

"Bailey, that you?"

Damn. I sagged in relief. "Marner, what are you doing here?" And how fast could he leave because I was *tired* (insert whining voice here).

"I was worried about you. It seemed like when we left lunch you were just a little, ah, not yourself." He stepped into the glow of my front porch coach-lights.

I snorted. "I was trashed. I don't do red wine well, apparently. But I'm recovered now, thank you."

He nodded. "That's good. I'm sorry about that. I never dreamt two glasses would set you buzzing."

I still wasn't sure if two glasses was the truth, or he didn't want me to know I had pounded three or four. "Yeah, well, I'm a light-weight, I guess. My Irish ancestors would be ashamed."

"It's because you've lost too much weight."

So we were back to that.

We were hovering in the drive and he didn't seem to have anything else to say, glancing to his right and staring at my porch. His jacket was off, and his sleeves rolled up, but he still wore his tie. Nothing was coming out of my mouth either now, because I felt brain dead and in desperate need of bathing.

"Can I come in?" he asked after a long minute of inspecting my tidy boxwoods.

No. But since I had interrupted his life by bugging him about Ryan and had asked him to compromise his professional ethics with the request for the report, I couldn't say that out loud.

"Sure. Do you mind if I take a five-minute shower? I feel gross." The humidity had been in overdrive today, even for August.

"No problem. Take all the time you want."

Leading him toward my front door, I rattled the pizza box in my hand. "Did you eat dinner? I've got pizza. It's cold now, but we can throw it in the oven while I'm in the shower."

"Great. I never got around to eating." Then he grinned as we stopped on the front step. "I've got the rest of that wine in the car if you'd like a glass."

My lip curled automatically. "Ugh. Never again. Never ever

for the rest of my natural life will I drink Chianti. You should be grateful for that fact, since I'm a sad drunk. How many times can I cry on you in one day?" Ramming the key in the lock, I sighed when my purse fell off my shoulder and hit the door with the force of a sledgehammer.

"You can cry on me whenever you want, Bailey. Really. I don't mind."

In all these years, I had never really noticed how *nice* Marner was. He had always been a bit like mild salsa next to Ryan's five alarm. There, but not really noticeable. Not in a grab-your-attention kind of way. But this was nice, having someone care enough to want to check up on me. I hadn't given him enough credit.

"You're sweet. Most guys would be running from me right now." With a yawn, I lead him inside, flicked on the lights and went straight back to my kitchen.

"This is a nice place. I haven't been here since you moved."

"Thanks." I like my house. I had been there about a year, and I was the first owner after it had been extensively renovated down to the studs. Not moving into someone else's dirt really appealed to me, yet I liked that they had retained or recreated the original charm wherever they could. Besides, it had an excellent floor plan, with a first floor guest suite and home office, plus my master bedroom upstairs with a glorious walk-in closet, so hard to find in an older house.

"When the little oven light comes on and it makes a beeping sound, you can put the pizza in." I turned the oven on and pulled out a cookie sheet. Trying to gauge Marner's hunger, I looked at the seven remaining slices. And put all seven on the baking pan. He was a guy, after all. "I'll be right back."

Fifteen minutes later, I returned, pleasantly clean and sleepy, wearing a T-shirt and soft cotton shorts. I had flicked the blow dryer over my hair so that it wasn't dripping, but it was still wet, combed straight and tucked behind my ears. Marner was sitting at my vintage French cherry breakfast table.

The pizza was arranged on two plates, one with two slices, one with five. Each pale green plate sat in the middle of a placemat, and my God, he had pulled two cloth napkins out of the basket and put them to the left of the plate. Goblets filled with ice water graced the upper right of each mat.

A man who knew how to set the table.

Actually, there were probably a fair number of men who knew how to set the table, but one who actually *did*, well, that was a novelty in my world. And he was a cop. Whatta ya know.

"Wow," I said. "Look at you, Mr. Domestic."

He shrugged, yanking at his tie as he leaned back in the chair. "I'm almost thirty years old and I'm single. I had to figure out how to take care of myself somewhere along the way."

That thought did a tired woman damn good. A man who could cook and clean and appreciated neatness? It was... charming actually. His mother deserved mad props.

The tie went over the back of his chair, and he leaned against it, which would cause a multitude of wrinkles before the night was over. I sighed. It really had been too good to be true to think he would match my anal expectations for tidiness.

"So no girlfriend these days?" I sat down and shook out my napkin.

"No, none to speak of. You?" He took a bite of pizza.

"I haven't been mentally stable enough to date." I said it in a light tone, but Lord knew there was truth to it.

He frowned. "Listen, the reason I'm here is because you caught me off-guard earlier with all the questions about Ryan's death. I've been thinking about it all afternoon, and I really hope that you'll just drop the whole thing. Let it go."

Not what I wanted to hear. Nor did I really feel like arguing about it. But I needed Marner for information so I couldn't just smile meekly and agree to drop it.

"Who would want to kill Ryan?" I asked, making clear my position.

His jaw moved while he chewed. There was no doubt in my mind he wasn't pleased with my question. His black eyebrows furrowed, and he got deep frown lines on either side of his mouth. "No one. Anyone. Cops have enemies, but then again, even *you* could have a stalker kill you without a soul ever knowing he was watching you. It *could* be anyone. But it's no one, because Ryan killed himself."

He believed that. Or wanted to anyway.

"Why would Ryan kill himself?" I asked softly.

"I don't know, Bailey. I just don't know." Marner's eyes were bleak. Miserable. "But that's what the facts say—you saw the report. We have to accept that. We're alive and he's not."

I almost blurted it out then. A sort of *hey, what if I told you Ryan was a ghost?*

But I kind of thought Marner would check me into a hotel without windows, where everyone wears pajamas and is fond of pink and blue pills. The supernatural and Marner just didn't go together—sort of like Jennifer Lopez and Ben Affleck way back in the day (what *had* they been thinking?).

"You can't ever really know what's going on inside someone's head," he added.

"What's going on in yours?" I asked, because I really didn't understand where he was coming from. Why was he so resistant to just looking into the possibility of murder?

"You can't even imagine what's going on in my head."

I had a feeling Marner had all kinds of secrets. Look at the whole cloth napkin thing. Who could have known that about him? If you gave me twenty tries, I could probably never guess what was on the bookcase in his apartment. Wrestling magazines? Hemingway? Harry Potter? I had no idea. Maybe he didn't even have a bookcase. I'd never been to his place. Not that he was eccentric, he was just, well, closed. Quiet.

"Okay, I get your point. But sometimes the way you feel doesn't make sense—and I feel that there is more to what happened than meets the eye." I sipped my water and waited for him to sigh. Reprimand. "It seems to me that everyone was awfully quick to just assume it was suicide without bothering to investigate whether it could have been murder."

I got the sigh. But no reprimand. Instead he just said, "Eat your pizza, Bailey. I'll look into it, all right?"

"Look into it?"

"Yeah. I'll look into it. Do some investigating."

"I could help," I offered, feeling guilty again for involving him. "To save you time."

His opinion of this was clear in the look of utter disbelief that flashed across his face. "Uh, thanks, but I'm good on my own. Never did like working with a partner, and you are not a cop. You stick to staging houses and I'll look into this."

Well. That was rude. But no less than what I expected. "I *was* an evidence tech, you know."

"Yeah, and you sucked at it, no offense."

"I did not!" There was a difference in hating it and sucking at it. "I have an eye for detail. I rocked swabbing blood and collecting fibers. I just didn't like it."

"I stand corrected." He sipped his water and stared me down.

Geez Louise, the man was intense. Time to switch tactics. "What happened to Ryan's car?"

It was hard to hold my eyes that wide, in imitation of my client Christy, but I was hoping to throw Marner off the scent. I don't do innocence as well as Double D Christy, apparently, because Marner was on to me.

"Why?" He moved on to slice number two, but still managed to sound suspicious around a mouthful of cheese.

"Uh...no reason." Channeling Flight Attendant Barbie, I smiled. "Just wondered."

"Stop wondering and stay out of it, Bailey. I said I'll look into it."

"Umm-hmm," I said, in what I hoped could be interpreted as a murmur of agreement.

Then I rammed pizza in my mouth and hoped Marner had Fridays off so he wouldn't notice me hanging around the station asking to see DeAngelo. That might make him just a little irritated, and I wasn't sure what exactly Marner would do when irritated.

Definitely not something I wanted to find out. The number of people I could flag as a legitimate friend on my phone weren't all that many.

I had to hold on to all of them, even the dead ones.

Chapter Five

W HAT DOES ONE wear to pump a cop for information? Slut clothes came to mind, but I don't own any slut clothes. Ninety percent of my wardrobe is business coordinates, and I couldn't imagine DeAngelo getting turned on by a sleeveless polka dot blouse with black pants. I bet he was the leather lace-up bustier type.

Then again, he had hit on me at Ryan's funeral, when I was wearing a black suit, black winter trench coat, and a voluminous ivory scarf. Snow boots, leather gloves, and an ivory hat had completed the ensemble, until the only thing visible had been a strip of my forehead, my eyes, and a bright pink nose.

Maybe he had an Eskimo fetish.

At any rate, I was not looking forward to our meeting, and Ryan wasn't here. It was ten in the morning already, and no sign of him. I had left Alyssa in charge of the staging at Tim and Christy's after staying up until two in the morning to create a design for her. I was exhausted, but I had put on a clingy sleeveless sweater, hoping that would prevent DeAngelo from dismissing me on sight, without actually arousing his interest. Emphasis on the word *without*. I did not want to be doing any arousing in relation to DeAngelo.

He had an ick factor of about three thousand on a scale of

one to a hundred, though I had to say, he was ahead of Detective Cox for the simple fact that he wasn't married.

I wanted to be smart and savvy, the girl who solves the crime while wearing shoes that wouldn't destroy the arch of my foot or somehow clash with my pseudo-red hair. In childhood my mother had lamented that ninety percent of the color wheel was off-limits for my ginger-ness, and that mantra had stuck with me. So with the clingy peach sweater, I put on fitted beige pants and neutral Jimmy Choo sandals that had been an indulgence for my birthday. Jewelry caused a major mental debate, and I finally settled on a cuff bracelet and tiny diamond studs. You could never go wrong with diamonds—perfect for a dinner date or crime solving, wherever your day took you.

Sitting in my car in the police parking lot, I took a deep breath and called Mrs. Conroy, Ryan's mother.

"Hi, it's Bailey. How are you?"

"Oh hi, hon. You're so sweet to call. I'm fine, how are you?" Mrs. Conroy had the kind of attitude that I wished I could have. She approached everything with faith and a smile. The quintessential housewife, she was like June Cleaver with soda bread recipes. Unlike my own mother, who had a cutthroat career as a prosecutor, Mrs. Conroy divided her time between church and her grandchildren.

"I just wanted to let you know that I think Ryan's house looks fine. You've kept it really clean and it's a starter home with first-time buyers, so I think it will sell soon." I didn't have the heart to toss Ryan's possessions or to let his parents pay for furniture rental for staging.

"I'd rather you just do your thing. I watch HGTV. I know how this works."

Home flipping shows were both the reason I had a business and the reason I couldn't keep most clients out of my designs. Everyone was an armchair decorator now. The love of hardwood floors and stainless steel appliances had to have an endpoint presumably, but that day was not today.

"I can go ahead if you want, Mrs. Conroy, but please, I don't want a commission. I'm doing it for you, and for Ryan."

Usually this was where my throat closed up when we had this discussion, but today I felt lighter, more at ease, because I still had Ryan. I could talk to him. Help him. Do something besides stagger through my grief.

"You're a sweet girl. Ryan was blessed to have a friend like you, and I'm sure from where he is in heaven he knows it."

Okay, I'd given up one guilt for another. Instead of feeling responsible for Ryan's suicide, I now felt horrible that I knew what no one else knew. While it might ease Mrs. Conroy's mind to know that Ryan hadn't committed suicide, I'm sure it wouldn't thrill her to learn he had taken up residence in purgatory, with no ticket to heaven anywhere in sight.

I made one of those murmuring sounds of agreement, grateful we weren't discussing this in person where my blush and guilty darting eyes would scream *Liar, Liar, Liar*. I really was a horrible liar.

But wait a minute—I knew from my own Catholic upbringing suicide meant no ticket to the pearly gates. So why was Mrs. Conroy so confident Ryan had gained entrance? Interesting. But I had to assume that she was willing to toss theological tenets to believe he was in a better place.

"By the way, what happened to Ryan's car?" See how I just slipped that in there? I was so smooth.

"His car? Jake sold it for us. The money we got paid the mortgage for five months. Why, dear?"

"Oh, I was just wondering. I noticed it wasn't in the garage." Marner had sold it. That wasn't surprising, except he hadn't bothered to mention that when I had specifically asked him what happened to the car. *Note to self: Marner keeps things close to the cuff.*

My mind had been wrapping around something I had read, an article that talked about how the criminal will often return to the scene of a crime. Some people thought that was a myth, but others cited case after case where the bad guy showed up where he had killed his victim, at the funeral, or the victim's home.

"I'll have the staging done by the weekend so your agent can do an open house." That wasn't usually how I worked with real estate agents. Normally, we had the house ready Monday or

Tuesday for professional photos, then the listing went up on Thursday, open house on Sunday, then an agent open house the following Tuesday. This was a rush job, but the agent was already bringing clients through the home so I wanted to get it looking its best to take advantage of every person going through the house. An idea had occurred to me that maybe, just maybe, Ryan's killer would find it amusing, titillating, to walk through Ryan's house.

That was assuming the killer knew Ryan, and had planned his death to some extent. But I couldn't see how it could be an accident. Who would be in an isolated part of the park with Ryan? Who would think to write a text if the crime was spontaneous? Actually, maybe that made it more likely. The more I thought it over, it made sense that a total stranger would show up for a gruesome thrill. If Ryan's killer knew him, he wouldn't risk showing his face at Ryan's old house.

So many ways to look at it. I chewed my fingernail.

Showing up at the open house to watch for a killer might be a dumb idea, but it was the only one I had.

"Sure, sounds good, Bailey. I'll call Rose and ask her what time so I can get the house aired out and cleaned right before. There's nothing worse than a stale house."

I could think of a lot worse things. That probably made me a pessimist.

"Great. I'll make sure there are scented candles." Got to have the house smelling like apple cinnamon for the killer, you know. Wouldn't want his nose to curl in displeasure.

My stomach did a loop-de-loop in disgust and fear. I so was not cut out for this.

DeAngelo met me in the front lobby.

"Well, well," he said, with a nice big smile.

Now you know when a man starts a conversation with "Well, well" that he just doesn't take you seriously.

"Look who came to see me twice in two days. Little Bailey."

Obviously we both knew I had been there the day before to see Marner, but I let it ride.

Those dark eyes gave me the once-over. "You've lost weight."

I needed to print that on my business card. *I'm Bailey Burke and I've lost weight. I know I look like crap, you don't need to point it out, and as soon as my throat resumes its normal swallowing function, I will regain ten pounds, so back off.*

But that probably wouldn't fit in the allotted space.

"I like it. You look hot. Like a supermodel."

Well. DeAngelo thought I looked good. Somehow that wasn't the slightest bit reassuring. "Thanks."

"What brings you by? Aren't you busy putting it here, or whatever."

I really had misstepped with the name of my business. "I need your advice."

"Why, did you kill somebody?"

There was no time for me to reply before he rocked back on his heels and gave me a wink. Not a "fun uncle" kind of wink, but a "give you five bucks if you lift your shirt" kind of wink.

"Not this time." I smiled tightly. It really was unfair that out of an entire station filled with decent men of high moral integrity, I got stuck dealing with DeAngelo of the offensive flirting.

"I know—you couldn't stop thinking about me and how much you want me." This statement was capped off with big black eyebrows going up and down.

I can't joke about things like that. This is why I was never popular in school. My distaste is stamped on my face clearly for all to see. And as an adult, I think I use my fakeness all up doing my job and there's none left for my social life.

Fortunately, DeAngelo wasn't a subtle guy. He didn't seem to notice that I was fighting the urge to roll my eyes and tell him off.

"Actually, I'm writing a book." I managed that with a straight face, even though the whole idea made me want to giggle. I'm the least likely person to have an interesting hobby. Bailey Burke, aspiring author, just didn't sound right. Closet writer didn't sound good either. I didn't do anything in the closet that wasn't in the pursuit of function and preventing fabric creases.

"And I was hoping you could help me make it realistic." This whole tactic had been Ryan's idea. It never would have occurred to me to do anything but blunder in there and ask questions about Ryan straight out.

Which was why Ryan had been a cop and I was a home stager.

But Ryan hadn't reflected on my complete inability to act or lie. I was rocking back and forth on my heels and gripping my purse like it would levitate if I didn't contain it. I suspected there was a weird, twitchy grin on my face.

DeAngelo just looked at me. "A book, huh? What kind of book? Is there sex in it?"

"Oh yeah. Lots of it." Then it occurred to me that could be misconstrued. "But I don't need help with that. There's a murder, which is why I'm here."

"What else is there in life? Sex and murder." DeAngelo shrugged. "Sure, I got five minutes. Come sit down and lay it on me. We'll fix you up."

I wiped my sweaty palm on my pants and followed him. I was terrified he'd figure out I was lying, only I wasn't sure why. So what if he found out I wasn't writing a book? What the heck could he accuse me of—wasting his time?

Yet nonetheless, I was scared shitless. Rules are good. Lying is bad. Naughty girls get punished. Therein lay the sum total of my parents' child-rearing philosophy.

Taking a seat behind his desk, DeAngelo tugged at his three-button shirt to get more comfortable. Thankfully, Marner was nowhere in sight.

"So who we killing, Bailey?"

"A hooker," I said, because it was the first person that came to mind after a cop, and I certainly couldn't say that.

"Gotcha, good. Hookers are easy." He winked. "In more way than one."

"Heh, heh," I said weakly, forcing a smile. "The murder is execution style. In a car."

"Oh, messy, messy," DeAngelo said. "I never suspected this

side of you. You look so prim, and here you are bumping off hookers. After they have lots of sex, huh?"

My trembling hand made me crave a hit off my electronic cigarette. But I could only smoke if I left the building, and I needed to stop using it as a crutch anyway. I took a deep breath. "Well, you know, we all have our dark sides."

"I like your dark side. So the druggie boyfriend did it, right? He's pimping her out, they fight, he taunts her, makes her drive him to a private spot, then he sticks the gun to her head and blows her away." This was accompanied by his fingers imitating pulling a trigger, and the very classic sound of *ka-pow*.

"Exactly! How did you know?" I pulled that exclamation off pretty good. Mentally picturing myself with big breasts and Cindy's pouty lips helped.

"Because it's goddamn obvious, that's why. If you're going for mystery, you should make it one of her clients. Like the mayor or something. The mayor, who doesn't want anyone to know he's paying for sex from a trio of hot, twenty-something professional cheerleaders."

What? Where did he come up with that?

He rubbed his mouth. "I'm liking this story better already."

"But how would the mayor get away from the car without someone seeing him? And wouldn't he be covered in blood?"

"The closer the gun, the less spatter and blowback. If he were in the backseat, he'd have some blood on his shoulders, his hair."

Eww.

"You should have the mayor take her out of the car and shoot her from about ten feet. It does the job and he'd stay clean."

"But I wanted the police to think it was suicide." There was no way I could actually pull an effective pout, but I did blink a bit, like I was distraught.

"Then that wouldn't work, because the powder burns would show the distance of the bullet from the impact."

"And how would he get away?"

"Second car, no doubt about it. He gets in his car and drives away."

"When people kill themselves with a gun, do they usually stick it in their mouth, or point it at their head?"

"Both. But most suicides with firearms are men. And the gun is always right against their head or rammed up in their mouth. Makes a big nasty mess. Like with Conroy."

While grateful he had brought up Ryan first, I didn't understand how he could be so freaking nonchalant. Had he hated Ryan? Or was he just so immune to violence that he'd forgotten people had feelings?

"How did you know for sure that Ryan killed himself?" I held my breath when DeAngelo gave me a funny look. For a distraction, I fiddled with the neckline of my clingy sweater. It worked. He glanced down at my chest.

"He was alone. No other prints on the gun. No tracks in the snow to indicate another car, or a walker leaving the scene. He made a will, went to a secluded place, sent his mom a text. The wound was self-inflicted, consistent with him being right-handed, directly into the skull."

I almost jumped but I managed to stay still. Ryan was left-handed. How could one of his co-workers not know that?

"What did the text say?" I asked, my throat squeezing and my stomach clenching. It did sound like suicide. Maybe I was crazy, imagining Ryan was here, talking to me.

"What?" he asked, stroking his five o'clock shadow, still staring at my sweater.

"Maybe if he weren't staring at your tits he would hear what you're saying," Ryan muttered in my ear.

Only by extreme willpower did I not wet myself. But I did let out a yelp and lifted my ass right up off the chair.

"What the hell's the matter with you?" DeAngelo asked, looking bewildered.

"Didn't mean to scare you," Ryan said, when I chanced a glance over my shoulder. "Sorry I'm late."

Yeah, sure.

"Bailey? What are you looking at?"

"Uh…something…bit me."

"Bit you?"

"Yes." I swatted my hand around my shoulder, whacking the space Ryan was occupying. It wasn't as satisfying as hearing skin crack on skin, but it was something. Ryan dodged me with a grin. "There's a big, nasty fly buzzing in my ear and it just bit me."

"I'm jealous of the fly," DeAngelo said with another of those winks he was so fond of.

"Oh, Jesus Christ," Ryan said, with a heavy eye roll.

My thoughts exactly.

"So anyway, what did the text to Ryan's mom say?"

"It said, 'I can't do this anymore'. Real chatty, huh? Guess Conroy didn't have a whole lot to say before he went out."

Ryan tensed behind me. "That's bullshit. Complete bullshit."

"When someone dies, how do you know that they made a will or something like that? I mean, like for example, how did you know Ryan had a will?"

"My girlfriend told me she did one for him right before he took his last little drive. She heard about his death on the news, called me and told me she'd just met him two days before when he'd come in requesting a will."

"Who's your girlfriend?" I asked, curiously.

"Deanna Adams. She has a law office right across from the station. But hookers don't have wills, Bailey. Trust me."

"He's doing *Deanna*? DeAngelo has a hot girlfriend? No way! There is no way she passed on me for him. That's like passing over Chris Hemsworth for Adam Sandler."

Ryan was flattering himself on the Chris Hemsworth comparison, and I was attracted to him. Plus if he didn't quit yammering in my ear, I was going to have to get up and move. I couldn't hear two people at the same time and know what the heck was being said.

"Are you still together? With Deanna?" At one point I'd thought I couldn't be any more grossed out by DeAngelo, but it turned out I was wrong. Now I knew he had asked me out when he was dating another woman.

"Yeah." He leaned back. Smiled. "But don't worry, we have an open relationship. She wouldn't mind me going out with you."

Eww. Double eww.

"No, thank you. I can only take one guy at a time."

Wait. That didn't sound right.

DeAngelo grinned. Ryan gave a choking laugh.

"Territorial, huh? That's sexy." DeAngelo leaned forward.

The horrible feeling came over me that he was going to touch my arm. No part of me wanted flesh on flesh contact with him. So I slammed myself back into my chair.

"Geez, freaking relax. I'm kidding," DeAngelo said. He laughed. "Come on, I'm not like that. Deanna is a cool chick. You know my flirting is harmless, right? I don't actually mean anything by it, and I don't want you to get the wrong impression."

What, like I would be disappointed? "Got it. Glad to hear it. Congrats on your relationship."

"He is making that up. There is no way Deanna, the hot attorney, is having sex with him." Ryan was clearly focused on a different part of DeAngelo's revelations.

Me, I was focused on the part that was leering at me.

"So how would my killer fake the suicide of the hooker?"

"He, or even she, if we're going with the mayor, would have to get dirty. Because if you kept the door open and did it from outside at a distance, to keep the spatter down, well, then, there's no spatter on the door or window and it looks weird, tells homicide the door got closed after the wound was inflicted. So you gotta keep the doors closed, duck down, gun to head, pull the trigger. But someone would fight you unless they were scared out of their mind. Or drugged. So you got to keep it all inside, stage the scene by wrapping the victims hand around the gun, then dropping it. Then walk away."

Ryan sucked in his breath.

"Covered in blood?" I asked. "How could you stroll away with blood all over you?"

"Winter or summer?"

"Winter."

"So your shoulders got some blowback. Take off your sweatshirt, mop your face and hair for any stray bits, stuff it under your coat you left on the floor of the backseat, and you head home to take a shower."

"But tire marks. Where did the tire marks go?"

"You're starting to piss me off, Bailey. You're making it too complicated."

"But you told me it would be better if it were complicated," I said in exasperation. The quizzical, trusting, bimbo persona was too hard to maintain. DeAngelo was getting on my nerves. The station was quiet, aside from the occasional chatter or loud laugh, and I felt smothered between two homicide detectives.

Ryan was breathing down my neck, figuratively, since he didn't actually have air to create breath. And DeAngelo was doing a scootcha-scootcha thing with his chair so that his knees were touching mine.

"You're smarter than you look."

Was there really any good response to that? I managed a "thanks" while Ryan cracked off a hearty laugh.

"All right, damn, so you're saying there's snow? But we can't have tire tracks? Well, the mayor didn't fly away. If there are no tire tracks, no footprints, no bike tracks, pristine snow, than your little escort really did kill herself. It wouldn't surprise me, you know. It's hell to be a hooker in Cleveland in the winter. Giving blow jobs with ear muffs on screws up your equilibrium."

"Um…" No words came out as I visualized this. Then promptly wished I hadn't. "Well. I guess I'll have to rethink things."

"Give me a call if you want to rework your story. Or if you need help researching those sex scenes."

I couldn't help myself. "Can you research sex scenes?" I asked with another dose of wide-eye innocence.

DeAngelo laughed. "Anytime you want to try, I'm more than willing."

Realizing I should have just dropped it, I gave him a glare. "You just said you have a girlfriend!"

"It's a joke. Have a sense of humor. Laugh sometimes. Eat a burger."

That did make me roll my eyes. I gave him a quick thanks and beat it out of there.

Ryan followed me to the parking lot. "I need the autopsy

report. My cellphone records. And you need to talk to the couple who found my body."

"Good morning, Ryan. Nice to see you too." My hands were still shaking and my deodorant had failed. That had been a highly traumatic conversation for me, and Ryan was all business. I didn't need a sticker or a cookie or anything, but a "nice job" would be appreciated.

Though I wouldn't say no to the cookie. That should make everyone damn happy.

He didn't catch my sarcasm. "Get in the car. People are going to think you're nuts if you're standing around the parking lot talking to yourself."

With a sigh, I got in the car and rolled down the windows. Ryan did his pop in trick and settled into the passenger seat.

"You know, this would be easier if you had come back as a dog or something. Like Benji. Then I could talk to you without people thinking anything of it."

Ryan gave me a grin, his hair falling in his eyes. "You'd pet me, wouldn't you?"

After a gasp, I tried to feign nonchalance. Ryan didn't know just how badly I had wanted to pet all his parts at one point in time. "Probably. People pet dogs. They're cute. I like cute things. I'd look mean if I never petted my dog in front of people."

"Would you rub behind my ears...or my belly? Would I be talking or just barking? It all sounds kind of kinky to me."

Picturing a little dog nuzzling into my lap, I cleared my throat. "Maybe you're right. It's fine like this."

Things were weird enough already.

Foot on the brake, I shifted to reverse. "So where does one find cellphone records?"

"At my house." He put his hand over mine. "And you're doing good, Bailey. We're piecing it together."

"Nancy Grace, that's me." I took my foot off the brake.

"Look out!"

My car connected with something solid and we came to a very loud, bumper-grinding halt.

"Oh God, what did I hit?" I asked, throwing the car into park and turning around frantically.

Ryan gave a choked laugh and shook his head in disbelief. "Just the chief of detectives."

Chapter Six

"WELL, THAT WAS really embarrassing," I said to Ryan an hour and a half later when all the paperwork had been sorted out from my fender bender and I had handed over my insurance information. As I headed across the parking lot for the second time, the midday sun had me digging for my sunglasses.

"If you're going to have a traffic accident, you might as well do it in the police station parking lot. Cuts down on your wait time."

We were clearly both pretty philosophical about the whole thing.

My phone rang. I checked the screen. "Hey, it's my sister calling from Texas. Let me grab this."

"Hello?" I leaned against my no-longer-perky SUV. The back end looked like a crushed soft drink can.

"Hey, cutie, what's up?" My sister Jen chirps when she talks on the phone. She has one of those personalities that are always set on high energy and loud volume. She is never angry, never cries, and has zero competitive drive. She also has a nice, albeit boring husband, four kids under the age of six, and a suburban house in Dallas.

Not a desperate housewife in the least, she thinks that my life will have no meaning whatsoever until she sees me happily reproducing like her.

"I just had a car accident, nothing major, but I'm tired from all the paperwork and stuff. Can I call you back tonight?"

"Geez, sure. But before you hang up I wanted to let you know I told a friend about you and he'll be sending you a message. He's really cute and his name is Ted. He's an accountant in Rockwall."

Deciding to play hopeful, I asked, "And he's transferring to Cleveland and needs me to recommend a great real estate agent for him and his wife?"

"No, you goof. He's single and veeerrry interested in you after I showed him the picture of you on your website. I figured you can chat on social media and in text or whatever and get to know each other. With your favorite sister giving you an excuse to come down to Texas every couple of months, there's no reason this relationship couldn't work."

It was all so simple to Jen. I guess technically it could work if I wanted it to. Except for maybe a million reasons. Starting with my love for a dead man complicating any blossoming amore with Ted, the Rockwall accountant. "Jenni," I said, because she hates it when I call her that. "I appreciate the thought, but please don't direct single men to my website. I don't need help finding dates."

"When was the last time you went on a date? Seriously. When Jasmine was born?"

Jasmine was my six-year-old niece. "Hey! Now don't be insulting." I turned slightly so Ryan couldn't hear me. He was sitting on the hood of my car, looking thoughtful. Probably not even listening, but it paid to be cautious.

"There was David." For a minute, I had almost even thought I could fall in love with David, the electrical engineer.

"That was two years ago!"

Picky, picky.

"You have got to get over Ryan, Bailey. I'm serious. It is *so* not healthy for you to still be pining over him."

I wasn't. Sheesh. Obsessing maybe, but not pining. Pining was pathetic. Obsessing was pro-active.

"Gotta go, Jenni. Love to you and Doug and the kids."

"Call me tonight," she yelled. "And remember the time difference."

"Got it." She reminded me she was on Central time every single time we talked. I'm sure that in the grand scheme of things one hour made no difference in the time-space continuum, but Jen seemed to think so.

"How's Jen?" Ryan asked when I hung up, his eyes closed, face tilted back to the sun like he could actually feel its warmth. Hell, maybe he could, for all I knew.

"Good. She had another baby. Finally got a boy."

"What is that, like her twelfth kid?"

"Fourth. They're still sticking to the "J" theme. Jacob joined Jasmine, Jessica, and Jordan."

"Wow. Or should I say *jeez*."

My thoughts exactly. "All right, let's go. I suck at this crime solving thing, don't I? Two days and I've accomplished nothing except to get drunk and hit the chief's Honda."

But Ryan didn't leap off the hood. He just shook his head. "We know a lot more now, babe. A lot more."

"I don't know anything." Truer words were never spoken.

But an hour later the one thing I knew was that Ryan's organizational system was about as bloated and illogical as the US government. There were six—count them, six—boxes of receipts, paid bills, and old bank checks rammed into a closet in his basement like it was 1999. In these very large, very heavy, bins o' crap, we were supposed to find the single cellphone bill from the month he died, which Ryan was about fifty percent sure "would be in the front box".

"Haven't you ever heard of a filing cabinet? Paperless online billing, for goodness sake?" I asked, my neck screaming in agony from being hunched over for thirty minutes straight sifting through the mess one piece of paper at a time.

It didn't help that Ryan was bodiless, and unable to move objects. Couldn't pull his weight, if you will.

"I don't like giving out my bank account info online."

"What are you, my grandmother? It's perfectly safe."

"They invented chip cards because it wasn't, and that still doesn't prevent fraud."

He did have a point. My eyes landed on the item in my hand, quickly scanning it. "Motts applesauce, bananas, frozen foods, frozen foods, frozen foods... Why in the hell do you keep your grocery store receipts? And why do you eat like a twelve-year-old?"

Ryan gave a shrug. "Stop judging. And I don't know. It's a receipt. You keep receipts. Stop wasting time reading stuff like that. You know what a cellphone bill looks like and it doesn't look like that."

He was taking a tone with me. I was sure it was because he had to just stand there, pacing back and forth, glancing at the items on top. But there was no need to get cranky.

"I'm just saying that a little organization wouldn't hurt. I mean, why is this check for The Bounce House stuck inside an electric bill? And what *is* The Bounce House?" That sounded just wrong to me.

"That's where I get my hair cut," he said, with perfect nonchalance.

"Your haircuts cost two-hundred-and-thirty-seven dollars? Wow. Maybe I should change careers." To exotic dancer, which had to be the service offered by something called The Bounce House.

He actually had the nerve to shrug. "They let me run a tab, then I pay every six months."

"You are such a liar." I shifted through a stack of bank statements. Ryan ran his checkbook a little close, month to month. He needed help creating a budget and some decent banking software. Or he would, if he were still alive. I sighed.

"Fine, you caught me." With a grin, he shook his head. "That was for the uh, *entertainment*, for a bachelor party. One of the detectives got married last year. Poor sap."

"What's wrong with marriage?" I asked, suddenly melancholy.

"Nothing, if you like being nagged and only want to have sex once a month."

I didn't see what was wrong with that. Once a month would

actually be a statistical improvement for me. One hundred percent. "How many times a month were you having sex?"

"Please." He gave me that bragging man look. "On average? Five times a week."

"Considering that you were usually with me at least three or four days a week, you are seriously lying." I dropped the pile of bank statements. "You know, how do we even know your mom put the phone bill in here? The bill would have come after you died, not before."

Ryan gave me a blank look. "Oh. Damn, you're right. I'm losing my edge. All this screwing around up there, filing paperwork and taking classes, has my brain turning soft."

I stood up, cracked my back and neck, and reached for my purse. "We should have done this in the first place." Plucking a phone bill for the wrong month out of the neat piles I had started to create, I dialed on my own phone.

Five minutes of hold music later, I had a rep asking if he could assist me. "Hi, this is Mrs. Conroy. My son passed away last February, and we closed his account. But I need statements for January and February to file his taxes. Our extension from the IRS only goes until August fifteenth, so can you fax those to me?"

"Account number, please."

I read it off and smirked at Ryan, who looked amused.

"Can you confirm your address and the account holder's mother's maiden name? Which would be your maiden name, I guess." The rep chuckled.

Chuckling right back, I said, "My maiden name? Right, of course." Then I gave Ryan a pointed look.

"Fox."

"It's Fox," I said, wondering if I really sounded like a fifty-five-year-old woman, since this man had no problem accepting me as Ryan's mother. That was a creepy thought. Maybe premature voice aging would be an incentive to quit vaping once and for all.

After giving him Ryan's address and a fax number, cellphone guy assured me I would have it that afternoon, and I hung up, feeling rather impressed with myself. "It's being faxed to me."

I must not have kept the smugness out of my voice because he rolled his eyes at me. "Yeah, yeah, you're all that, Bailey. We got it."

"Do you want my help or not?" I asked, full of phony indignation.

Ryan gave me that goofy grin, where I knew if he had been able to, he would have grabbed me, tossed me under his arm, thrown me around a little, and ruffled my hair. He settled for twisting his features into gruesome contortions that made me laugh.

"I want *all* your stuff, baby." He rolled that right into a ZZ Top imitation. "Give me all your lovin', all your hugs and kisses too."

It made me laugh, despite the crick in my neck. "No kissing, sorry."

But suddenly he stopped playing air guitar and looked at me, puzzled.

"What?"

"I don't know... Something just flashed in my head, like a memory of something. But I lost it before I could put my finger on it."

Damn. My face flushed. What if he was talking about that kiss? I turned and started picking up the piles of papers and shoving them back into the box. "That happens to me all the time. Like a déjà vu thing. Maybe it will come back to you later."

Plunging me into hell.

"You're probably right. And I need to bug out of here. I'll catch back up with you later when you've gotten the phone records."

"When?" I asked, picturing Ryan popping into my bathroom when I was doing something unmentionable.

"I don't know. Call me once you've gotten it and I'll come over."

This gave me pause. "Call you? How the hell am I supposed to call you?"

"You click your heels three times and say 'there's no man like Ryan'."

"Not." That was so not happening.

76

"Okay, seriously, just call my cell."

"Your cell?" I raised an eyebrow. "The cellphone that was turned off six months ago? How could that work?"

"I don't know, but it does." He pulled it out of his pocket and shook it for emphasis. "They use it to call me all the time—I bet it works for you too, since you're my contact."

I wasn't buying it. So I scrolled though my contacts until I found his name. I had never been able to make myself delete it. "It's ringing."

A second later, Ryan's phone chirped a whimsical version of *Greensleeves*.

"Nice ringtone." And quite different from the no-nonsense flat out ring he used to have.

"Thanks. It fits the new image better." He swiped his screen. "Hello, The Grateful Dead speaking."

"You're so weird." Hanging up on him, I finished cleaning up the papers and shoved the box back into the closet and shut the door.

"That's why you love me, right?"

"No, I love you because I'm stupid." Which was as close to the truth as I was willing to skirt.

"You said it, not me." Ryan threw his phone up in the air and caught it. "Hey, what would happen if I tossed my cellphone to you? I mean, is it real or is it a ghost phone?"

"I can only imagine."

He arched it through the air. It hit my arm. Not as a solid mass, but as a wisp of air as it passed through my skin. My flesh. My bone. And dropped onto the ground.

I yelped.

"Whoa," Ryan said. "That was a little weird."

"A little?" I grabbed my chest, rubbing it to encourage my heart to start beating again. "Don't do that again."

Bending over, he scooped up the phone. "Maybe I should have read my manual a little more closely. Some of this stuff is probably explained in there."

"Manual? What, like instructions for the afterlife?"

"Yep. It's a textbook that came with my Intro to Death class.

But you know I don't read anything that isn't Sports Illustrated. So I haven't really checked it out yet."

"Why don't you do that tonight?" The mere thought of proceeding without directions had my shoulders stiffening. I am a slot A into slot B kind of girl. Give me a step-by-step and life is good.

Without directions, there is only chaos.

Ryan just rolled his eyes. "I'll skim it if I have time."

"Like you're so damn busy?"

"I got class tonight, I told you that."

Then he blew me a rude, obnoxious, sexy, smacking kiss and he was gone.

I was left with boxes of receipts, growing confusion, and a desperate sense that my life as a babbling, eccentric spinster had just begun.

Marner was in my driveway again when I went home to check my fax for the phone records.

"Shoot." It couldn't be good that he was sitting there at two in the afternoon. Easing my SUV snugly behind his truck again, I decided to pretend like I knew nothing about anything. Ever.

"Hi," I said brightly, smiling with teeth as I stepped out into the driveway. "What brings you by? Late lunch? How about Chinese today?"

My clever ruse of distracting him with food didn't work. Probably because I sounded like a demented Barbie. And the breathy voice didn't suit me. For me to act sexy and perky was like raising a guilty flag.

He had gotten out of his car immediately, though he was looking at the sky. I got the feeling he was counting in his head. Or praying.

"Bailey?" His voice was very, very even. Quiet. Hard.

He sounded so much like my father I almost said, "Yes, sir." Fortunately I caught myself and said, "That's me."

"Why the hell were you at the station today asking DeAngelo how someone could fake a suicide?"

"Um…" I dropped the faux cheeriness. "Look, don't be mad at me."

"That would be the understatement of the goddamn year." Even as his fists clenched, his voice stayed low and deadly. His jaw locked into a scowl and I became aware that he was much taller and much stronger than me.

I decided that he would be a very scary cop to encounter in a dark alley when you'd ticked him off. It wasn't a stretch to picture him unleashing that contained fury to the serious detriment of the ticker-offer. Without even realizing it, I stepped back a foot and clutched my Burberry purse in front of me.

"I'm writing a book."

"What?" Incredulity crossed his face and his shoulders relaxed a little. "You don't really expect me to believe that line you fed to DeAngelo, do you?"

"No." I sighed. Turned my sandals a little on the concrete and opened my purse. This called for a hit on Skinny Winnie, which was the utterly ridiculous name I had given my electronic cigarette. I spoke down into the depths of my purse as I searched for it. But of course I didn't have it, because I was determined to quit so it was at home. But what I did find was gold. It was an old pack of actual legit cigarettes. Apparently I hadn't used this bag in quite some time. There were two still inside it. I drew one out and stroked it like a kitten's fur. "I'm sorry, I wasn't trying to stir up trouble or anything. I just thought that DeAngelo could tell me some things about Ryan. But at least I was discreet."

That earned me a snort. "Yeah, sure, discreet my ass. DeAngelo's telling the whole damn station that you're writing a book about sex and murder and asked him for help with both."

"Ah!" Abandoning my search for a lighter, I glanced up in horror. "That's not true! I was just asking about murder that looks like suicide. He offered his help with my sex scenes, which I turned down, several times and he said he was joking and that he has a girlfriend. He wasn't much help, honestly."

"Because there is no book."

"No. I turned him down because I can't even fathom acting out anything sexual with that guy." Holy crap, I found a lighter in the exterior pocket of my purse. I lifted the cigarette to my lips, not even sure why I was doing it other than the undeniable—I was nervous, exhausted, emotionally drained. And possibly going insane. There was still no actual proof that 1) Ryan had committed suicide and 2) that his ghost was actually appearing to me.

"But there is no book." It wasn't a question.

"No," I admitted sheepishly.

"I said I'd look into the case. You could have trusted me to give you answers, not go to a loose cannon like DeAngelo, for Chrissake."

The case. He meant Ryan. Confident that Marner had released most of his anger, I studied him. "You won't tell me everything, Marner, and you know it." My words were muffled because of the dangling cigarette, but still decipherable. I flicked the lighter and nothing happened. The filter tasted stale in my mouth but I forged ahead. "Would you give me pictures of the scene?"

"*Hell no.*"

"Would you give me the autopsy report?"

"No." His shifted from one foot to the other, looking stubborn and appalled.

"Do you believe me that it could have been murder?" I tried to light my cigarette again but Fate seemed to be telling me to knock it off.

"No. I don't believe that."

"I rest my case." I flicked the lighter for the third time and the wind blew out the flame. "Damn."

Marner reached out and snatched the lighter from me. I thought he was going to toss it into my bushes or something, but instead he just cupped his hand up next to my cigarette to shield it from the wind and used his other to flick on the lighter. Startled, I just stood there for a second, staring at his chest, aware that his leg was bumping mine. Then my cigarette caught, I sucked in with gratitude, and he moved away, dropping the lighter back into my purse.

"Thanks," I said, feeling guilty and not sure why. It had been Ryan's idea to see DeAngelo, yet I felt like I had betrayed Marner. Hurt him. I blew out the smoke. Holy tobacco. The smell was overpowering, as was the rush of nicotine.

"Did DeAngelo give you crime scene photos, the autopsy report?"

"No." I watched the tip of my cigarette burning next to my thigh and wondered what to say. I settled for, "I'm sorry. I'm not trying to cause trouble for you."

He sighed. "Did you ever think there might be a reason I don't tell you everything? Like maybe I'm trying to protect you?"

That pricked my independent woman nerve. "What decade is this? I don't need to be protected."

"No? Well, have it your way. Before he died, Ryan was having a relationship with a former prostitute. And the autopsy showed he was using."

"Using what?" I sputtered. A prostitute? That was a disgusting visual. Was Marner insane?

"Using *drugs*, Bailey. Remember that knee surgery he had last summer? Well, from the toxicology report it looks like he was abusing his pain meds. He had a shit-ton of Vicodin and Xanax in his system. Why do you think the department kept a tight lid on info about Ryan's death? We were trying to prevent the media from catching wind of any of this. I'm sure Mrs. Conroy would not appreciate hearing on the evening news that her son was popping pills and hanging with a hooker."

Even as I shook my head and tried to form words through my shock, I knew this was wrong. It had to be wrong. Ryan didn't say anything about a prostitute. And drugs? That was ridiculous. "Marner…"

He put his hands on my shoulders and leaned in closer. His voice was soft, soothing. "I'm sorry. But it's true. Good people get hooked on that stuff. It doesn't change anything about how we should remember him."

I tried to say something, but only managed to make a choking sob. I felt two tears trickle down my cheeks.

"Shh." His thumbs wiped my cheeks. "It's okay. Ryan made some bad choices and sadly, he paid the price. But he was still Ryan, and he was my friend, and I am going to protect his family. But you need to find some way to move on, babe."

He'd never called me babe before. It was Ryan's nickname for me.

"Marner…" No other words were forming. I felt just heartsick, scared. If what Marner was saying was true, than I had to be imagining Ryan. But I couldn't be imagining Ryan. It was too real, and I wasn't that crazy. Hovering a bit on the edge, but not completely out to lunch. Which meant the only other alternative was that Ryan was lying to me. "No."

"Bailey." Marner wrapped his arms around me completely and pulled me against his chest. My cheek squished against his jacket, my lip hitting the smooth button on his white shirt. I lay there, numb, not sure what to do.

"We'll never know for sure what was going on with Ryan, but obviously something was wrong if he was using and involved with a woman like Hannah, who knows every drug dealer in town. Sometimes there just aren't any answers and we have to accept that."

His hand was rubbing my back and I felt disconnected from my body. Like I was floating over myself, dizzy and spinning in circles. It had to be the nicotine. I let the cigarette drop from my fingers onto the driveway. Smoking it wasn't satisfying. It didn't have the same thrill it used to. Now it felt like I was trying too hard.

"I'm sorry, Marner." I wasn't sure what I was apologizing for, but it seemed important to say that.

He must have understand I meant for the whole situation en masse, for the cold lonely fact that where we'd once been three, there were now only two of us. His lips brushed the top of my head.

"I know, babe. I'm sorry too. Sorrier than I've ever been."

Chapter Seven

I STILL HAD work to do, so after Marner left I trudged inside my coral Victorian and into my home office. Spinning my chair in circles, I took in my idea boards, my inspirational art, my charcoal velvet drapes. I needed to concentrate, but I felt aimless. I needed to talk to Ryan and see what the story was. Someone was lying to me, and I had a sinking, horrible feeling it was Ryan.

Why wasn't a ghost around when you needed one? So annoying.

Forcing myself to make a few phone calls, checking in on Alyssa and Jane at the Jensen project, and ordering some furniture online, I remembered what Ryan had said. I could call him. It had worked when he was standing next to me. Maybe it wouldn't now, but it was worth a shot.

I swiped my screen and found his name. I called and held my breath, waiting for the ring. It worked, even though his phone had been turned off.

After three rings, he answered. "Yo, Bailey, what's up?"

Relief and anger rushed through me simultaneously. "I need to talk to you."

"Well, you called me. So talk."

"Can you get down here?" Or over here. Or whatever we were supposed to call it.

"I'm kind of busy right now. I have exams coming up and

they're giving me crap that if I don't pass I can't move on to the next level." His voice was low, like he didn't want to be overheard.

"I thought once we solve your murder you're supposed to be able to move on." I stared at my screen saver until my eyes blurred. I didn't know what to think anymore.

"I guess I have to pass the classes too."

That made me frown. "You lied to me," I said. "Marner said there were drugs in your system at the time of your death."

The silence was so long I knew it was the truth. "They were from a doctor. I had residual pain from the stupid knee surgery. What difference does that make?"

I closed my eyes and tried to center my thoughts. Swallowing, I opened them again, determined to get this conversation over with. "Because it was way higher than any acceptable limit. Plus you were taking anti-depressants. Which is fine if you had a prescription from your doctor. But you can't tell me with any certainty that you didn't actually pull that trigger. You must have been high as a freaking kite." I felt betrayed and I wasn't even sure why.

Guilt was there too. That Ryan had been struggling with both depression and pain and an addiction to painkillers, and I hadn't known. He had been battling his demons silently, with a cocky smile.

"I know what I know and I didn't do it. It doesn't matter that I was popping pills. It's not like I was buying them off the street, and frankly, it's none of your business."

"So you weren't buying them off the prostitute you were seeing?"

He got defensive. "And that's *really* none of your business. That's my personal life. I don't need your judgy bullshit. Just because you're wound so tight your ass squeaks doesn't mean that you have the right to criticize someone else. Hannah is a decent person who has turned her life around."

I was so stunned I didn't know what to say. For a second I just sat there, stiff, fighting off the urge to cry. Finally, I spoke softly, as calmly as I could. "I've never judged you. That's not what any of this is about. I'm trying to figure out what the hell really happened that day, because that's what you asked me to do. That's all."

But it was also about the realization that I'd never had Ryan and I never would. His heart had never opened to me the way I wanted. He liked me. He cared about me. But he could never love me—I just wasn't his type. He didn't like squeaky asses.

Ryan swore under his breath. "I'm sorry. I didn't mean to be such a dick."

Actually, he had, and I wasn't sure why. What sore spot had I touched? Maybe he loved Hannah the Hooker. Maybe Hannah was a lovely person. That wasn't the point. What was relevant was he had me running around poking my nose into police business and all of it might be completely unnecessary.

"I only mentioned her because I thought maybe she was supplying you with painkillers. But okay, fine, you don't want to talk about it, that's cool. I have work to do," I said. "And I'm upset with you right now and I don't like feeling this way about my dead friend so I'm going to have to go."

"I get it."

That was it. He wasn't going to explain anything.

I didn't want to ask about Hannah but I couldn't stop myself because I'm a glutton for punishment. "Do you love her?" I asked softly. "Maybe you should have appeared to her instead."

"No, I don't love her, though I might have eventually."

There went the knife, twisting into my heart.

"I don't know how it would have played out. But I came to you, Bai, because you always have my back. That's everything."

His response brought the tears that I'd been holding at bay rolling down my cheeks.

That meant more than he would ever know, because I wasn't going to tell him. "Yeah. I do. But don't call me Bai. You sound like a teenager." It was a source of contention between us that had grown into a joke. He used the nickname because he knew I hated it.

"Bye, Bai. I'll catch you later."

The call ended and I stared at my phone. I went into my call log and saw there was no record of Ryan and I talking.

It made me want to lift my e-cigarette to my mouth and suck on it like a catfish with algae. Fighting through it, I stood up and went to the kitchen for some cheese and crackers. At least my appetite seemed to be returning.

Maybe my squeaky ass would fill out (clearly I would not be over that particular remark anytime soon) and everyone would be happy.

~

My appetite had actually returned with a vengeance. On Saturday I kept my promise to Alyssa to hang out, but we skipped the movie. I ate my way through the day as we wandered around Ohio City poking in shops.

"I feel like I'm making up for six months of not eating," I said. We had started the afternoon out at the West Side Market, a huge hundred-year-old indoor market with stalls selling every kind of food you can imagine. I had eaten a crepe and then an hour later a meat pastie. After hopping one neighborhood over to Tremont to shop the boutiques, we got goat cheese guacamole for a snack. Because, well, goat cheese guacamole.

Now after a tapas dinner, we were packing it away at Mitchell's, a locally made ice cream served up in a shop that was formerly a vaudeville theater. I had an amazingly creamy Tin Roof sundae with Spanish nuts on it. It was heaven in a dish. Despite being full, there was no stopping me now.

"I think you needed a high-calorie day." Alyssa had a cone and she delicately licked it.

Alyssa and I had met in calculus class in high school, and she was basically my complete opposite in every way, right down to her platinum hair against my auburn (okay, so in adulthood it was more like brown with hints of red). Alyssa was easygoing, casual. If she dropped ice cream on her pants she would just shrug. But we had bonded over music and our love of pretty things. Her personal style had a more modern meets retro flare, whereas I was classic and tailored. Today she was wearing a vibrant print sundress and very large, very yellow earrings.

Shockeroo, I was wearing simple black pants and a white shirt. It was the handbag and shoes that made an outfit in my book.

"Yeah, but I have a food baby." I rubbed my now-round belly and groaned a little. "Everything in moderation is clearly not my motto."

Alyssa, who had voluptuous curves, and rocked them, shrugged. "Who cares? Sometimes you need to go with your gut. Literally."

All day I had been debating telling her about Ryan. It didn't feel right though. It would cause tension while she debated my sanity.

"I know, but I'm probably going to be up all night with heartburn."

Alyssa glanced behind me and nodded a little in the direction she was looking. "Some guy is coming over, by the way. He's super hot. Like, I'm going to lick this cone and pretend it's him."

That was hot. I turned to catch a glimpse of this panty-dropping paragon and was startled to see Marner, dressed in a T-shirt and jeans, his biceps on full display. He had a new tattoo on his forearm I hadn't known about—a Celtic cross. Which was weird, given that he was Italian. I could see how Alyssa would think he was good-looking. He looked imposing. Confident.

"Hey, Bailey." He pulled a free chair out and sat down next to me. "How are you?"

I gave him a genuine smile. "I'm fine." I was, surprisingly. "This is my friend Alyssa." I turned to her. "This is Ryan's old partner, Marner."

"Nice to meet you." Alyssa was practically drooling. She flicked her tongue suggestively over her scoop.

Okay, then. That was annoying, though I wasn't sure why. Alyssa was entitled to think he was hot. And come to think of it, he was entitled to respond if he wanted to. But he didn't seem to notice. He was inspecting my sundae.

"You put a nice dent in that. Good job."

That made me roll my eyes. "Thanks, Dad." But then I felt like a jerk, so I asked, "Are you here alone? Cruising for a scoop?"

"I'm actually heading next door for dinner. I happened to see you in the window and I just thought I'd say hi."

"Hi." I waved. He was an attractive guy. I had always known that, in theory, but Ryan had managed to out-charm him. Or maybe Ryan was just an attention hog. But after the other day, when Marner had held me yet again, I had a case of the warm fuzzies for him right now. So I smiled.

His dark eyes widened slightly. "So have you two eaten dinner? Why don't you join us? My buddy Nick won't mind."

"Is he single?" Alyssa asked. "Because Bailey needs to start dating."

Really? I glared at my friend.

"Oh." Marner looked taken aback. "Actually, he is. Want me to put in a word, Bailey?"

"No, I do not, but thanks though." I felt my cheeks turning pink. "Alyssa doesn't know what she's talking about. I don't need to be fixed up with strangers."

His eyebrows rose. "How about with people you know?"

I had no idea what he meant by that. Fortunately, before I could get flustered any further, Alyssa spoke again. "We already ate about six times today, but we'd love to join you for a cocktail, Marner."

"Call me Jake."

Wait. What? She got to call him Jake after two minutes? I had known him for seven years. *Years*, people. He had never once told me to call him by his first name. Not that I would anyway, but I should have the option.

Alyssa beamed. "Great."

If they started dating and got married and had children I was going to puke.

But when we stood up Marner pushed my hair out of my eye. "You look good," he said. "Really good."

A shiver went through my body from his unexpectedly gentle touch. For a split second I felt it actually reverberate through my lady parts, which shocked the hell out of me. Maybe I had gotten more than my appetite back. "Thanks. I feel pretty good."

I did.

Nick turned out to be a fun guy, and the four of us passed a great hour just talking about sports and food and normal things. Not about murder or death or ghosts. Imagine that.

It also seemed that despite Alyssa's initial thought to thrust me at Nick, an investment banker Marner knew from college, he was actually hitting it off with her. At one point they were leaning in to each other and laughing and Marner glanced over at me.

"I don't think Nick's joke was that funny," he said. "But someone sure does."

I sipped my iced tea. No wine for me this time. "Someone likes someone."

The look Marner gave me made my heart rate kick up a notch.

"Yeah. Someone does like someone," he murmured.

What the heck did that mean? Was he saying…

His finger came out and swiped at the corner of my mouth. He took the tip to his lips and sucked. "Sugar," he explained.

I tried to laugh, but it was caught somewhere in the back of my throat along with the question that I was dying to ask. Was he hitting on me?

There was no way. Just no way. Way?

Marner winked at me and I wondered when exactly the whole world had gone mad.

But this change I actually kind of liked.

Chapter Eight

MRS. CONROY'S FRIEND, the real estate agent selling Ryan's house, was a woman who also knew my mother. I had thought she had looked familiar the other day, but I had been too out of it to ask her name. When I arrived at the open house at Ryan's we chatted for a few minutes. When she introduced herself as one of the Murphys from the Irish-American club, I remembered that before I had discovered competitions make me cry, I had gone to dance school with her daughter, Bridgid.

Cleveland Irish are a close-knit interwoven group of descendants with a particularly high concentration from two counties in Ireland—Clare and Mayo. Traditional Irish blessings still hang over fireplaces, soda bread is still baked, and the Celtic Festival and the Kamm's Corner Hooley (which I think is Gaelic for big ol' party) are events not to miss. Long before Riverdance made it A Thing, second or third generation moms enrolled their daughters in Irish step dance classes, carefully choosing schools based on where they themselves had danced as a kid.

By three or four years old, girls were jigging and reeling their way across the stage at festival and competitions, me included. By five you're wearing a wig full of faux Irish curls and your mother has glued your knee socks to your legs so they don't droop on stage. There is such a thing as roll-on sock glue, believe it or not.

The ultimate goal of all this seems to be a championship dancer who will give her parents an excuse to travel to Ireland for Worlds.

Bridgid Murphy had been a great dancer, making her way up the ranks of the competitive levels. I was a great dancer too, but I cried a lot. I was in love with the wigs and the shoes and the elaborate embroidered dresses and the blingy brooch that clipped to my cape. But one wrinkle, one crease, one spilled juicebox on my dress and the waterworks opened. Commence screaming and crying.

Hey, I like things tidy and I was born that way. I was a hard worker though, and by solid effort and constant practice, would place at competitions. But I was such a neurotic mess when I didn't win first place (because, hello, that means you're the *best*) that eventually by the time I was thirteen my mother pulled the plug on my championship dreams, sick of sacrificing Thanksgiving dinner every year for me to compete in the regional competition, the Oireachtas, in Chicago. Then watch me cry when the results didn't go my way.

In hindsight, I wasn't sure how she had tolerated a decade of that with me and my sister. Jen never cried, but she also never put any effort into it. She was stuck at novice level for years and could have cared less. My mother's reprimands to me were "Jesus, Mary, and Joseph, stop crying, you took second place!" To my sister they were more along the lines of "Lazy girls finish last!" Something of a mixed message, but my sister and I were opposites.

Mrs. Murphy told me Bridgid had gone to Worlds and was now a certified teacher with her own school. I was impressed. "Wow, that's so great. Tell her I said hi."

The open house was just getting underway and it was already hopping. I wandered away so she could monitor the activity and speak to potential buyers. The house looked ready for the market. I was pleased with the end result of two days of chaotic staging. The rooms bore no resemblance to the way they had been when Ryan was alive. I had banished the plaid to a storage unit and brought in mid-century furnishings with narrow legs to make the small rooms seem larger than they were. It also was a modern nod to the architecture of the home. It had been built in 1964 for this exact type of furniture, not giant chunky sofas.

I hadn't seen or heard from Ryan since I had called him. I wasn't exactly sure how I felt about that, and I wasn't sure if me being at the open house was to see the fruits of my labor, or to follow up on my idea that if he had been murdered, the killer would show up. I had done some further research and that sort of only seemed to apply to serial killers, which I was certain wasn't the case with Ryan. Besides, I wasn't convinced at this point Ryan had even been murdered.

Knowing that Ryan had been dating someone at the time of his death did make me feel suicide wasn't as likely, but then again, depression and pain had nothing to do with anyone other than the person experiencing them. Yet I felt uneasy given everything DeAngelo had told me about the difficulty of faking a crime scene. Add in the addiction to painkillers and suicide seemed like a real possibility.

It was with that thought that I wandered around the house Ryan had been mostly ambivalent about, if I were honest with myself. He had bought it as an investment and put little time or effort into it. It was me who got sentimental over real estate. Under other circumstances (as in, before his ghost appeared) I might be reminding myself that he was no longer here. A house didn't contain a soul. But the irony was that of course I kept looking over my shoulder, waiting for him to pop up out of nowhere and scare the crap out of me.

Crazy lady talks to herself at open house. That would be classy.

It wasn't Ryan who popped up though, but a guy I vaguely recognized. He was in his mid-thirties, muscular build. He smiled at me. "Bailey, right?"

He knew my name. "Yes." Here was the awkward "Do I know you?" moment. I couldn't place him.

But he caught on without me having to ask. "I'm Caleb. You probably don't remember me. I was a beat cop when you worked in the department."

It clicked into place. "Right. Oh sure, hi. How are you?"

"I'm thinking about buying a house. Would it be weird if I bought Conroy's?"

Yes. But I just smiled. "It's a great deal." It was. "Are you single, or do you have a family? Either way, it's a perfect first house."

He shook his head. "Just me. But I'm looking for an investment. I'm going to look around." He touched my shoulder. "Good seeing you."

"You too."

Caleb wandered back toward the bedrooms when DeAngelo walked through the front door. What was this, a curiosity for cops?

He waved at me when he came in and I felt my eyebrows shoot up. "Hey," I said, as he came toward me. "Are you in the market for a house?" Maybe the women in evidence would show up next, geez.

He made a face, glancing around the living room and open-concept kitchen. "No, no, not at all. I don't like commitments. I'm more of an apartment kind of guy. I came because I was hoping you'd be here. I wanted to talk to you."

Weird. "You could have gotten my number from Marner." Wait. What was I thinking? I did not want DeAngelo to have my number. There was no telling what kind of memes that man would feel compelled to send me. You know, as a joke. *Just kidding, Bailey. Lighten up.*

DeAngelo gave me a funny look. "He would never give me your number. Trust me."

"Why not?" I was bewildered as a young couple brushed past me with murmured apologies. They looked twelve, but were wearing wedding rings. I suddenly felt ancient.

"If you don't know, don't worry about it." He rubbed the back of his head. "That's not the point. Look, so if you're serious about writing that book, I have an idea of how murder could be made to look like a suicide."

That piqued my interest. "How?"

"Someone makes the victim kill himself."

"Who would agree to shoot themselves?" My God, that was a horrifying image.

"Someone who knows that whoever is in the car with you already did something horrible, like killed his kids. Or they know they're going to die no matter what. Look, if I had a gun to my head and they told me do it yourself or we'll do it, then go and kill your family, I'd eat a bullet. Don't mess with my family, you know?"

So DeAngelo had a family. I'd always assumed he'd crawled out from under a rock. I was starting to think that wasn't fair of me, though. Maybe he wasn't a bad guy, just one with a juvenile sense of humor. There were worse things. I needed to give him the benefit of the doubt since he seemed inclined to help me. "Okay. But that means they would have to have a lot of power over that person, right?"

"I would say so. The threat needs to be taken seriously."

Who would Ryan feel genuinely threatened by? A drug dealer? That seemed possible. But I still felt uneasy. I just didn't know what to believe anymore. "Under what circumstances would you fight back?"

"I would say most. Because you know you're going to die, you might as well go out fighting. Unless, say, they had my girlfriend with a gun to her head. That's totally different. I'd have to stay cool."

I hadn't thought about that. "Interesting. What if the dead guy is an addict?"

DeAngelo's eyebrows shot up. "An addict? Well, then, what the hell are we debating? Someone buying drugs is a sitting duck. Overdose them then use the victim's finger to pull the trigger. Boom. Lights out before they even know what hit 'em. Literally."

That was what I was afraid of. Damn it. This was all so complicated. It could genuinely go in either direction and I didn't know if I could believe Ryan or not. Maybe he just didn't want to admit he'd killed himself.

"Wouldn't that be bloody? Wouldn't there be gaps in the blood spatter?" I knew it would disrupt the pattern from my brief tenure as evidence tech.

"Then we're back to forcing the victim to do it." DeAngelo shrugged. "I still like the mayor getting whacked better."

"Thanks, I appreciate you helping." I heard the real estate agent discussing a potential offer with the young couple. It made me happy to think a young family would buy the house. But then I heard the husband ask, "Did the owner kill himself here in the house?"

"No, it wasn't on the property."

It was inescapable, discussions about Ryan's death. "I should head on out of here. I feel like I'm in the way." And I wanted some kind of closure, only I didn't know how to find that.

"I'll walk out with you. And you should give me your number so we can text if you have any other questions."

I glanced at him curiously. It seemed strange that he had just shown up to discuss my book with me. The book that wasn't ever going to exist. Maybe he really was just trying to be helpful. "Cool, thanks." I dug out one of my business cards. "So how's Deanna?"

"Good. We should double-date sometime."

Um, and who would I be paired with exactly? I pictured DeAngelo having a brother. I was trying to be more open-minded, but no thanks. Not happening. I made a noncommittal sound and checked my phone. Just a bunch of work related texts. I wasn't exactly burning up the social scene.

Then I got a text from Ryan.

Ask him about the file on my desk. The one about the retirement investments.

"Hey, um, what happened to the files on Ryan's desk? His mom said something about needing some information on the retirement investments." I tried to look nonchalant, but my palms were sweating.

DeAngelo's face went blank. "I don't know what you're talking about."

"That makes two of us." I was serious about that. I had no clue what I was talking about. "See you around, thanks for the ideas." I waved to him and walked down the sidewalk to my car. It was sizzling hot today and I pulled at my T-shirt as it stuck between my breasts.

Ryan started walking next to me. "You didn't exactly try very hard back there."

I glared at him. Then murmured under my breath, "I'm not discussing this with you. There are half a dozen people in earshot."

That was when I heard the gunshot.

I jumped and turned to see what was going on, instinct propelling me toward my car.

"Get down!" Ryan yelled.

Fear was pushing me forward, not down, but all of that was overshadowed by the fact that Ryan followed his own instincts and tried to take me to the ground with him. Only when he went to grab me, he went *through* me. Intense cold seemed to invade my body from the inside out and a shiver rolled up my spine. It was like being shoved into a walk-in freezer, then immediately yanked back out. The sensation was gone almost as soon as it began, but the shock and discomfort lingered.

Ryan was on the ground, staring up at me, looking equally stunned. "That was disturbing as hell," he said. "Holy crap, Bai, I've been inside you."

It had been both intimate and invasive and his choice of words was truly unfortunate. But it was all irrelevant, considering there was an active shooter in the area. Chancing a glance behind me as I jumped over Ryan's prone ghost body, I reached for my car door. DeAngelo was in the neighbor's yard, talking to a man, looking unconcerned. He saw me and waved, though I wasn't sure if it was a wave to reassure me, a wave to go over there, or to take off as fast as I could.

"What am I supposed to do?" I shrieked at Ryan as I got in my car. He was already in the passenger seat, which was annoying. His ability to transport had me genuinely jealous.

"Everything looks okay. Drive up to DeAngelo."

So I did, rolling down my window. My heart was still beating faster than normal. "What just happened?"

He strolled over, looking amused. "Idiot neighbor almost shot himself in the foot. He was cleaning his gun on his back patio."

Well, that was going to kill any potential sales from the open house. I grimaced. "Ryan's house is crawling with people. He could have killed someone walking in or out. Geez."

DeAngelo shrugged. "Well, he didn't. Relax, shorty."

Shorty? Every time I made an effort to like DeAngelo, he just verbally vomited all over it. "I'm leaving then. See you around."

He waved and strolled down the sidewalk to his car.

"Isn't he going to report that or anything?"

When Ryan didn't respond, I turned to ask him again. Only he was gone.

Without any warning or a wave or a single word. I shivered, remembering the sensation of his energy passing through my body. I never wanted that to happen again. It had been too personal. Too real. Too much of a reminder that he had no physical body.

I reached into my glove compartment and pulled out my e-cigarette and took a tiny, guilt-ridden puff on it. Then I crammed it back in and slammed the drawer shut. I had dinner plans with my parents. Leaving my car in park, I closed my eyes and did a quick breathing exercise, trying to quiet my thoughts. You couldn't go into my parents's house frazzled. They would eat you alive.

Ready, I opened my eyes and started driving west.

If anyone ever wonders how I became the woman I am (as in, neurotic and the aforementioned tightly wound) they only have to spend five minutes with my mother and/or step foot into her house, to understand my evolution. My mother is a trial attorney, with no tolerance for emotion or laziness. I grew up in a suburban mini-mansion, with every inch tidy and clean and clutter free. It was professionally decorated, because my mother wanted perfection without having to think about it, and she had eschewed the nineties trends of red dining rooms and stenciling on walls for a classic look with wingback chairs and cherry wood furniture. Rarely did she move anything around, which drove me insane as a teenager, but that was the way she was. It was controlled, like her, and because she had chosen such quality furniture and classic colors, the décor was still in style.

My father is a pharmaceutical rep, with a boisterous laugh, and the red nose of his Irish heritage. He's charm to my mother's efficiency, and together they had conquered this thing called life in terms of money and material possessions. Presumably their marriage was mostly happy. When I was in the sixth grade, they had a rocky patch, with lots of screaming and threats of divorce, which had rattled my sister and I to the core. But then as gradually as it had escalated, it disappeared again, and we stopped holding our breath waiting for the divorce announcement.

Sometimes I wished my mother would knock back a bottle of chardonnay and confess what had happened, but that wasn't her. She was a lock box and no one had the combination but her. Unlike me, who wore everything on my face.

When I walked into the house, sweaty from the heat and humidity, my mother looked cool as a cucumber, a glass of iced tea in her hand as she sat in the living room reading on her tablet. She greeted me with a smile and a hello, but her eyes dropped to my chest, which had a damp spot between my breasts. Stress sweat. Ninety degrees and hearing a gunshot will do that to a girl, what can I say?

My grandmother, my father's mother, was knitting on the couch. She was ninety pounds soaking wet and barely five feet tall. She still liked to brag sixty years later that my father had been an eleven pound baby and she had him without a c-section. "You're looking a little better, sweetheart," she told me. "You've looked like hell the last few months."

She was also master of the backhanded compliment. "Thanks, Grandma. I think my appetite is coming back." Plus I was talking to my dead friend, but I would keep that little detail to myself.

"I'm glad," my mother said. "You can't let grief consume you."

Fairly certain that my mother had somehow managed to go through her entire fifty plus years of life without losing anyone particularly close to her, I thought that was a bit patronizing. But it's better to just ignore her. Let it go. Be Zen.

"Did your sister tell you the news? She's pregnant again."

"What, really? No, she didn't tell me." I sat down on the couch, lifting my hair off my neck and fanning myself. "Has anyone explained to her how babies are made? Because I feel like she has no clue. She always seemed startled when she turns up pregnant again."

My grandmother laughed but my mother frowned. "Don't be flippant just because you're jealous. Your sister has a beautiful family."

That made me laugh out loud. The jealousy part. Not the beautiful family. "I'm happy for her. I really am. But jealous? Eww. That's what I have to say about having four kids under the age of seven. Soon to be five. That sounds like hell, so trust me, I am not jealous. I don't even want to be married right now." Envisioning my future had been difficult when I had been focused on establishing my business and processing the fact that my fantasy of Ryan suddenly figuring out he was in love with me would never be realized.

"Are you dating?" Her eyes sharply took me in.

I had walked right into that one. "No." But Marner popped into my head, unbidden. I flushed, thinking about his thumb dragging across the corner of my mouth.

"She's lying," Grandma said. "It's written all over her face."

Which was astonishing, since she wasn't even looking at me. She was focused on her knitting. "What are you making?" I asked her. "That looks downright psychedelic." It was purple and pink with shots of silver.

"It's a sweater for you."

Oh. "Wow."

But then she winked. "Don't be so gullible. It's a blanket for the church raffle."

Thank God. I meant that quite literally.

"You really *are* gullible."

I jumped and let out a small shriek. Ryan was on the couch next to me. He was eyeing the tray of appetizers my mother had set on the coffee table. There was brie and crackers, olives, and prosciutto.

"What's wrong?" My mother looked at me like I'd grown two heads.

"I…had a cramp. A charley horse."

"Eat more potassium."

"Okay." I clenched my fists in my lap. I reached forward and grabbed a cracker to prevent myself from responding to Ryan. I wanted to tell him to knock it off. Popping in and out at random was rude. Just because he was dead didn't mean etiquette didn't apply. Send a text in advance.

"Don't be salty," he said. "I had a thought."

"That's a first," I said, before I could stop myself. I was salty and so what? Everyone else was allowed to be in a mood, but I expressed any emotion and it was all "Bailey's a mess." Cranky crank. That's how I felt.

"A first what?" my mother asked, looking at me curiously.

Um… "I've never had a charley horse."

She raised her eyebrows but didn't say anything.

"Where's Dad?" I asked.

"He went to the pre-season Browns game. I don't know why he still gets season tickets. It's like throwing money out the window. Or setting cash on fire."

"He's loyal. That's what fans do. They stick around through the bad years and celebrate the good with their team." I wasn't a die-hard football fan, but I figured if you were in, you needed to be all in. No fair weather fans. That amused me. There was, generally speaking, nothing fair weather about Cleveland.

"With this team, that's like waiting for a marriage to get better. Good luck with that."

I had no idea what to even say to that. I hoped it wasn't a personal reference. "He has fun."

"That's because he drinks."

God, help me be patient with my mother. I begged for serenity. "How's work?"

"I'm going to trial this week. Child pornography charges. Guy is a real sicko."

That wasn't anything I wanted to talk about either. "Hmm." I was distracted by Ryan trying to pick up an olive. He kept at it, repeatedly slipping right through the bite-size food. It was like watching a baby continually miss his mouth—I just wanted to help him. I also kind of wanted to just shove it at his lips to make him stop. "Mom, have you ever had a case the police initially thought was suicide but it turned out to be homicide?"

My mother paused in slicing brie. "No. You need to stop watching so much crime TV. Things like that don't happen very often."

"I don't think your mom ever liked me," Ryan commented. He went for the olive again. "How did Patrick Swayze learn to touch stuff in Ghost? I need to watch that flick again."

Life would be easier if I could speak telepathically. "I need to go to the bathroom."

I gave Ryan a "come with me" look.

He went into the powder room with me. "This is kind of kinky."

I turned on the faucet. "Can you please find something else to do? This is getting to be too much."

"I'm sorry." He crossed his arms. "Do you want me to go away and never come back?"

That instantly made me feel guilty. "Of course not! I mean, unless you've found your Higher Purpose or whatever we're calling it. I just think you need to contain it to my house. When I'm alone. Otherwise I can't say anything to you anyway and it's pointless."

"True. But it's boring to be confined to one location. Plus I'm getting ahead of myself. I'm excited. I remembered something. I saw DeAngelo lift some cash from a crime scene a few days before I got killed. It was a drug deal gone wrong and the victim had a bunch of cash, but the killer got interrupted. The guy had five hundred bucks on the ground and DeAngelo took a hundred."

"You think DeAngelo murdered you over a hundred bucks?" That seemed like a stretch.

"No. He killed me because I took his promotion. And his girlfriend."

"What?" He had lost me completely. Again.

"The girl I was seeing a year ago used to be with DeAngelo. She left him for me."

You know, I was a little bit tired of hearing about all the women Ryan had dated while I gave serious thought to getting a cat for companionship. Every woman in town had men falling all over her but me. I had Ryan running out of my house like a bullet shot from a rifle after I'd told him I loved him. Which might not be the best way to think of it. I frowned.

"That was a year ago. I doubt he laid in wait planning your demise. That's really melodramatic."

"I think there was no neighbor with a gun. I think he was taking a shot at you this afternoon."

"*What*?" That was impossible. DeAngelo liked me. Or at least wanted to do dirty things with me, which was kind of the same thing. He would not try to kill me in broad daylight on a Sunday.

There was a knock on the door. "Bailey, are you okay? You've been running the water for five minutes and now you're talking to yourself."

"I'm on the phone," I lied.

"Good Lord, Bailey Ann. What is wrong with you? No one should have to be subjected to speaking to you while you tinkle."

Ryan started laughing. "I love that your mother says tinkle. That just made my day."

I rolled my eyes. "I'm done."

"Then turn off the water!"

"Do you ever just wish that for once you could please your mother?" I murmured to Ryan. "Because I do."

"Nope. My mom thinks I'm the bomb."

He was right. His mother had worshipped the ground he'd walked on. "I think I have bad karma."

Ryan attempted to ruffle my hair. Nothing happened, of course. "You have a good heart. That's all that matters."

What I had was a lump in my throat.

He wasn't going to linger on the sentimental though. "You're right. I'm grasping at straws. Who would want to kill someone as awesome as me for a hundred bucks?"

"I can't imagine."

Chapter Nine

RYAN DIDN'T MAKE phone calls. That was what I learned from his cellphone records. His mother called him every few days and they would talk for just about ten minutes. Other than that, he never spoke on the phone. He texted, but not an above average amount. I had heard from him every few days. He texted Marner periodically. I recognized that number. There was one number he had texted extensively in the last two weeks before he died.

Probably the woman he had been dating.

It would have been nice if he had mentioned he was seeing someone. Then I would have kept my mouth shut and I wouldn't have endured six months of thinking I contributed to his suicide. But Ryan had secrets. That's what I knew now. We were friends, but that didn't mean I knew what was in his head or his heart.

I sipped my coffee in my home office and spun in my chair. I could never find an office chair I liked. They were either ugly and comfortable or beautiful torture devices. I had gone for attractive on this one and it did nothing to save my posture or wrists. Someone needed to invent a way to work while being massaged with virtual hands.

The only number on the call record that looked unusual was the very last one. There was an incoming text from a number that didn't appear anywhere else on the call log. Then Ryan had responded two minutes later. It would have been after he left my house, before the park. I decided to block my number and call it. Ryan had clearly decided to ignore the tiff we'd had and I really didn't want to dwell on it either. But I had no idea what to believe anymore. Logic kept telling me suicide was the only answer.

With clammy hands I entered the number on the phone record and waited for someone to answer. "DeAngelo," came a familiar voice.

Sucking in a breath, I ended the call. Ryan's last text was to DeAngelo. Aside from the one sent twenty-two minutes later to his mother. His very last text.

So did that mean it was DeAngelo Ryan had been meeting in the park? A text didn't prove that though, and there was no way to ask without gathering suspicion. I just couldn't find a motivation for DeAngelo to kill a co-worker.

"Ryan, if you're listening to me, this is a dead end. No pun intended." My voice rang loud in my quiet house. I usually had music playing in the background while I worked, but today I hadn't wanted to hear bouncy pop music. I had chosen silence and now it felt heavy, smothering. Clicking on the TV for background noise and company, I thought for a minute.

This was stupid. Maybe I needed to go back to the police station and just be bold.

Instead, what I did on total impulse was call up Hannah and arrange to meet with her. I had taken a guess that she was the number Ryan had been texting so frequently before he died, and when I dialed it, I was right. She was friendly and willing to give me a ten minute meeting. She chose a bar in Lakewood, ten minutes from my house. Not a crowded hipster haven like the one that had cornered the market on twenty-somethings by having retro arcade games. This was *actual* old school. A genuine corner dive bar that hadn't been redecorated in at least twenty years because it didn't need to be. It had its regulars who most likely who would balk at anything pretentious. There was one lonely pool table in the back and dinged-up barstools. The room smelled like grease and a faint hint of smoke, like occasionally the bartender puffed when the place was empty. Two weary looking men were at the bar, though they weren't sitting together.

Popcorn was set on the bar top every few feet, but I couldn't imagine digging my hand into a bowl where countless other hands had been buried. Hannah wasn't there yet, so I just sat down on a stool and ordered a glass of wine. It was the wrong choice. The bartender didn't say anything but it took her a minute to dig around in the cooler and find a solitary mini bottle of white wine buried in the back. This was clearly a beer bar and I was feeling self-conscious in my floral shirtdress. Not that anyone was paying me any attention.

My mother always told me I had an invisible audience and I was starting to think she was right. I needed to be more confident, especially if I was going to solve a murder. So I sipped my wine and resisted the urge to hide behind my phone screen. Instead, I took in the wall décor. It was mostly a mish-mash of liquor and beer signs, plus some sports memorabilia. LeBron James was staring down at me, sitting on a throne. A picture from BTD, Before The Decision. Before he broke the hearts of Clevelanders and headed for the sun and sand of Miami and a virtually guaranteed championship ring.

They needed an update. The image of him crying on the court after he kept his promise to win with the Cavs. Full circle. But then again, this wasn't an on-trend bar. Maybe they liked to cling to the underdog days, to the sense of grittiness that was at the heart of Cleveland's history. Maybe that wasn't a bad thing—respect the past.

My past was starting to feel like quicksand. The more I moved, the more it shifted and sucked me in. I wanted to move forward and heal. Not get pulled into acknowledging that everything I had ever known was an alternate reality. I was starting to understand this about Ryan and his life, not about me. I clearly hadn't even known him as well as I thought I had. My past was really the version of the truth I had chosen to believe—what was shown to me on the surface.

A woman came in through the back door, alone. She had on a Mötley Crüe tank top and skinny jeans with flip-flops. There were tattoos on both of her arms, and she had jet-black hair and bright-red lipstick. She was beautiful, her face both exotic and friendly. Her arms looked toned but not from working out, just from good genetics. Based on looks alone, she was definitely Ryan's type. I gave her a smile. "Hannah?"

She smiled back as she approached me. "Yes. You must be Bailey. Nice to meet you."

I tried to remember if I had seen her at Ryan's funeral, but there were so many people there and I was so distraught I didn't think I would have noticed her, especially in a winter coat and hat. "Thanks for meeting me. I'm sure you're wondering why I called." I waited until she sat down on the stool next to me. "But Ryan told me he cared about you and I've been thinking about him a lot and well, I just wanted you to know that you mattered to him."

Even though he had never mentioned her before her death. But now he had made it clear he cared about her, and had staunchly defended her.

Her eyes instantly got glassy. Her voice was husky, sexy. "He was a good man. I thought, you know, that maybe for once, somebody was going to love me for *me*, not for what they could get from me."

I saw it then—what would have appealed to Ryan. The vulnerability behind her probably usual bravado. I imagined they laughed at the same things, listened to the same music, drank the same beer. But she was a woman who needed protection, and he was the man who could provide it.

Yeah. He would have fallen in love with her and it actually made sense.

A flush crawled over my face, not because I was jealous or angry. But because I was too stupid to see it then. For years I had been trying to force an intimacy that wasn't there, and even if it were, would never work. Ryan and I were friends and could have never, ever been anything different. We just weren't alike, not in a way that would ever work for a relationship.

Heavy thoughts for a Monday. I should have ordered something harder. Like a shot of tequila.

"Losing him was hard. You're right. He was a good man." If he suddenly popped up behind us though and started eavesdropping I was going to be pissed. I gave him a mental warning to stay away. I wasn't sure it worked like that, but it was worth a try.

"So you were friends for forever, weren't you?" Hannah ordered a beer on tap.

"Yes, for about ten years. We're opposites, so it was kind of an odd friendship, I guess."

She eyed me curiously. "So you never did anything else?"

I shook my head vehemently. "Oh no. God, no. Not even close." I was going to say not even a kiss, but technically I might have done that, though it hadn't been reciprocated.

"That must be nice. I've never been friends with a guy who didn't want to get naked at some point."

I tried not to be insulted, because I knew she didn't mean it that way, but it was a bit of a kick in the pants. Though I was determined not to be so freaking sensitive again. Hannah oozed sex appeal. I didn't. I could change that if I wanted to. I am not exactly an ogre. Some might even call me cute. It was the lingering redhead syndrome. I had spent my whole childhood being called a Ginger and having my smattering of freckles made fun of. That's my story and I'm sticking to it.

"The thing is, Ryan and I were friends, but it was more of a brother-sister relationship. You care, but you don't share everything." I could see that clearly now. "I did want to ask you though if you knew anything about what he was doing earlier that day he died. Like who he might have been with. Maybe it was you?" I asked.

She shook her head. "No. I hadn't seen him in a few days, though we texted."

I knew from the call log that was the truth.

"But he mentioned he was meeting Jake."

Jake, as in Marner? Why was Hannah allowed to call him Jake too? What the actual hell? Then a more relevant thought occurred to me. "That morning? Or afternoon?"

"That afternoon. But it sounds like he never made it there."

So another dead end. "Anything else weird about how he was acting? Was he worried or upset?"

"No, not at all. He was excited about the money though."

That was news to me. "What money?"

"He said he was getting five grand from an insurance policy."

Now that was weird. Ryan didn't have a relative who had died and he hadn't had any damage to his house or car, so what else could it be? "Did he say what it was from?"

Hannah shook her head. "No." She grinned. "We were celebrating that night, not talking."

How magical for them. *Nope. Not jealous. Not me. All good here.*

"Gotcha." Hopefully there would be no forthcoming details. I really wanted to ask her about the prescription drugs, but I didn't see any way to approach that subject without completely offending her. "Five thousand dollars, huh? That's a lot of money."

After sipping her beer, Hannah made a face. "Sucks that he got killed and never got to enjoy it."

Hold it. "Ryan committed suicide."

She gave me a long look. "Whatever. I don't believe that for a minute. If you do, that's fine. But I don't."

"I don't know what I believe." That was definitely the truth.

My phone buzzed in my purse. I fought the urge to look at it. Business could wait five minutes.

Hannah's phone chimed in her hand. She did choose to look at it. Her face changed, growing excited, or at the very least distracted. "Sorry, I need to go." She drained her beer in one long gulp. "Nice to meet you."

Then she was gone. I realized that she hadn't paid for her beer, which was fine. I had invited her. It did seem odd she hadn't even offered. Turning her life around, maybe. But she was used to getting what she wanted from people. That was irrelevant though.

Sighing I pulled my phone out of my purse and glanced at the screen. There was a text from an unknown number.

Mind ur own business or you'll end up with a bullet in ur head 2.

~

I was in my house with the doors and windows locked, wishing I had installed a panic room in the basement, when Marner showed up. After checking to make sure it was him, I threw the door open and said, "I'm going to die," as a greeting.

He frowned, a crease appearing between his eyebrows. "Not today, if I can help it. Now calm down and tell me what happened."

After he stepped inside I made sure I bolted the door closed. "Look at this." I shoved my phone at him.

He read it, his expression never changing. "Did you try to text them back?"

"No! Are you nuts? What, like I'm going to engage with a killer? Antagonize them?" I sucked on my vape. I couldn't help it. I was terrified. I paced back and forth in my bare feet.

"There's no proof that a killer wrote this."

He had lost his mind. "So this is a random text from a random stranger? Completely unrelated to anything going on?"

"It's possible." Marner was wearing a suit and he peeled his jacket off and draped it over one of my living room chairs. "We can't jump to conclusions. Let me text them back."

I scrambled over to him and tried to grab my phone back. "No!"

He looked startled, but he let me take the phone. "Why not?"

"I'm scared." Maybe cops didn't get scared, but home stagers did. I could attest to that.

His expression softened. "Come here. It's okay." He pulled me over to him.

I resisted, because I was annoyed that he hadn't indulged me from jump. But he tugged harder and I gave in, letting him draw me against his chest. He smelled woodsy and sexy and I breathed deeply. There it was again. That weird tingling in places that shouldn't tingle in broad daylight with a man who wouldn't give me the right to use his first name.

"I don't think it's okay," I bemoaned. "I feel like something weird is happening. Who has my number? It has to be someone I know." That was a terrible thought. Who had my number?

Hannah. DeAngelo. Clients. The women I had worked with

in evidence. Marner. Out of that list, DeAngelo was the only who seemed likely to threaten me. It wasn't a comforting thought. Maybe Ryan was right—DeAngelo had meant to shoot me.

A shiver rolled down my spine. I glanced up at Marner. "Did you know Ryan got five grand just a few days before he died?"

"What? How?"

"Hannah told me it was from an insurance policy, but that doesn't make any sense to me."

Marner stopped rubbing the small of my back, which was disappointing. He set me back a little and frowned at me again. He frowned an unreasonable amount. "Why were you talking to Hannah?"

Oops. *Busted*. He wasn't supposed to know about that. I was seriously lousy at this whole investigative crap. "I called her and we met for a drink. It was a five minute conversation, honestly. But the relevant information here is she said that 1) Ryan was murdered and 2) she said he just got an insurance payout."

Marner seemed to be debating whether he was going to shake me or give me a stern lecture or just hand out the classic silent treatment. His jaw worked and he pressed his hand to his eye briefly, like it was twitching. "Why are you fixating on this? What has changed?"

Ryan appearing in my kitchen and asking me to flash him to check his arousal potential.

I wanted answers. Closure. But I wasn't getting the answers I wanted. I scrambled for a response to Marner's question other than "the dead speak to me." "I think it's just that now the shock has worn off. That's all."

He studied me so intently I almost squirmed. My arms were still loosely around his waist, my e-cigarette dangling. For some reason, I tucked it into his pocket. I wanted both hands free to squeeze him.

"Did you just put your vape in my pocket?"

"Yes. I'll get it in a minute." I rested my cheek on his dress shirt. It was crisp and cool. He wore a suit well. Working man meets GQ.

"I don't know what to tell you about Ryan, babe. I wish I did."

"Then tell me why you don't let me call you Jake."

He stiffened. Then he tipped my chin up so I was looking at him. "I never knew you wanted to call me Jake."

We were doing something again, like we had at the ice cream shop. There was a shift in the air between us. "I do," I said, and my voice was like Hannah's. Whiskey smooth, sexy. I ran my tongue over my bottom lip.

He dropped his gaze to my movement and his already dark eyes darkened more. "That's fine by me. And for the record, I'm glad you called me. Any time you're scared, you can call me."

"You really don't think I need to be afraid?"

"No. I don't. But I do think you should let me kiss you."

I could say I hadn't seen that coming, but that would be a lie. Marner had been inching toward this moment and I had been letting him. Encouraging him. Now I was surprised at how much I wanted him to close that gap between us. "I think I will."

He didn't hesitate, but he didn't hurry either. Marner was maddeningly intense, the way he always was. Deliberate, dedicated, diligent. His mouth took mine and for a split second I forgot everything and everyone.

Then I heard Ryan's voice behind my left ear. "Oh come on. Are you kidding me right now?"

I jerked back and shivered when I felt the cool space as I collided with Ryan's ghost form. Breathing hard, I put my hand on my chest. I refused to acknowledge Ryan because this had nothing to do with him. It had everything to do with Marner. *Jake.*

So to smooth over my sudden movement, I said, "I think I should let you do that again sometime."

"I won't object to that."

"Since when has this been going on?" Ryan asked. I refused to look at him, but I was getting a little desperate. He was destroying what was kind of an awesome moment. Marner was cupping my cheek with his callused hand and giving me that stare he was so gifted at delivering.

"Do you want to go out for a cup of coffee?" he asked. "Now? I don't have any plans tonight."

"That sounds great." I thought maybe if we left my house, Ryan would evaporate or whatever he liked to call it.

"You do know that Marner has back hair, don't you?" Ryan asked.

Shut up, shut up, shut up. Had he always been this obnoxious? Just because Marner was Italian didn't mean he had back hair.

Yet I found myself studying the nape of his neck for evidence of a carpet of hair descending below his collar. There wasn't one.

Marner was opening the front door for me. I took juvenile satisfaction in turning and sticking my tongue out at Ryan. He was just giving me crap just to be a jerk.

He ruined my gesture by laughing riotously.

Chapter Ten

THERE COMES A point when you have to stop being afraid. As I stood outside the police station, I told myself that time was now. Yet my heart was still thumping and my palms were sweaty. Marner had asked me to meet him there and after the other night, when we'd had coffee and conversation and some legitimate lip-locking on my front porch, I was worried about why he wanted to see me.

Was he going to announce to everyone we were dating? No. That was ridiculous. We're weren't dating. Yet. Besides, you didn't tell your co-workers about every twist and turn in your personal life. So maybe he actually wanted to let me down easy, tell me it was a mistake to kiss me. And do it in front of everyone, so I wouldn't flip out? Okay, my mother was right. I did take things to the level of ridiculous. No one fixated the way I did. It could be absolutely anything, and most likely something awesome and flattering, like he just wanted to see me.

Instead, as I sailed through the security check-in wearing flare leg jeans and wedge sandals (going for a sexier, bohemian, whimsy Wednesday kind of vibe), Marner met me with nothing more than a "hey." He didn't even notice my outfit, even though I'd left the top button of my shirt undone, or the blowsy-breezy effort I'd put into my hair and makeup.

He didn't touch me either. No hug, no hand tug, no rubbing of the back.

Deflated, I said, "Hey," in return and waited for him to backpedal. The old "I never meant for you to get the wrong idea" speech. You know the one.

Yet like so many other women before me who angsted endlessly over what a man was thinking, I was completely wrong as to what it was. In his cubicle he shoved some papers at me. "There was a five grand deposit in his account," he said in a low voice. "From a retirement investment."

That was both a relief (that he wasn't telling me to buzz off) and disturbing (because why did Ryan have five grand?).

So Marner had taken me and my hysteria seriously. Or he had been curious. Whatever the case, he had looked into Ryan's assets. "Maybe he wanted to go on vacation or buy a new truck." Ironic that I was the one now playing devil's advocate. But it didn't seem that suspicious to me if the money had come from his own account. People withdrew money all the time from their retirement investments. Hell, maybe Ryan was anticipating needing to buy pills when his prescription ran out.

"Except it wasn't his. It came from the account of someone else."

I glanced down at the papers. "Who is William Peppers?" I whispered.

"I have no idea. But this looks like insurance fraud to me, and no offense, but I don't think Ryan was smart enough to do this on his own. This is a white collar crime."

"I don't think Ryan was smart enough to do that solo either." I couldn't do it. Most people couldn't. It would take someone seriously tech savvy and devious to boot. "Can we trace it, like with IP addresses and stuff?" I had no idea what I was talking about, but that's what they would do on Criminal Minds. "Or maybe I can just look up who owns the company distributing the funds."

When I looked up from studying the evidence in my hand I saw the reaction I had wanted earlier, delayed. Marner was looking at me like he was on Day 18 of Naked and Afraid and I was a wild boar.

"You look very cute right now." He reached out and tucked my hair behind my ear.

Cute? Really? Yet I still flushed with pleasure. Hey, I haven't dated in a while and Marner could make you feel like you were the only human being in existence when he looked at you.

This was the tricky part of crossing that line of friendship with someone. There was no telling what we were actually doing at this point. So despite my inner squeal, I tried to play it cool. "I have a business meeting in twenty minutes."

"So what does that mean, you can't go to lunch with me?"

"No, I can't do lunch, but what I meant was I'm dressed up cute because I have a meeting."

He looked amused. "I wasn't talking about your clothes."

But he did step back and give me space, which I needed if I ever wanted to breathe again.

"Okay, I'll call you later," he said. It wasn't a question, because Marner didn't ask permission. I had already granted him permission when I had agreed to let him kiss me.

He was a wave I could get swept along with, and that made me nervous. Besides, I suspected we had the exact opposite reaction to the information that insurance fraud was in play. I was inclined to believe that Ryan had stumbled onto it after the fact. Marner seemed to think Ryan had been party to the fraud. It made me wonder what he had seen from Ryan on the job that I hadn't been privy to. A different side from the charming, carefree guy I knew.

"See ya," I said.

I stopped by the evidence room where techs were doing what I had once done—scanning fingerprints electronically, processing evidence to send for DNA testing, and generally pushing around paperwork. Unlike on television, it wasn't a glamorous job, and it didn't require a science or forensics degree. It was for criminology majors like myself who were detail-oriented and could handle the mundane nature of the daily grind. I could have stayed if it wasn't for the blood. And for the fact that when I was called to gather DNA, sometimes it was from a live human, and sometimes live humans protested. I hadn't appreciated being called a skinny bitch by a rapist. Just a little unnerving.

All of those feelings came back when I saw my old co-worker, Sandra, bent over a computer, doing data entry. She had a pile of bagged swabs on her desk next to her. She glanced up and smiled. In her late thirties, Sandra was a divorced mother of two and had a sharp sense of humor. She was immune to gruesome crimes scenes, and part of me envied it, but part of me was grateful I hadn't gotten jaded the way she had. But being a single mother made her pragmatic. She needed the job.

"Well, well, look who's here," she said. "I heard you and Marner were a thing. 'Bout time."

The curse of having fair skin and Irish genes is you blush the color of a ripe tomato. There is no hiding embarrassment. "Who told you that?"

"I heard DeAngelo and Cox giving Marner a hard time about it. He never admitted it, but he never denied, so that's totally an admission."

"I don't what we're doing," I told her truthfully.

"No one ever does." She twirled in her chair so she was facing me. "Guess what? I finally got my ex's ass into court. They're garnishing his wages. I can move out of my parents' house."

"That's awesome. I'm so happy for you." She had been working on that for at least a year. Her ex-husband had hooked up with a twenty-year-old waitress and gotten her pregnant. That was his argument for not paying child support for his existing kids—he couldn't afford them now that he was having another one with a virtual teenager. "I'm sorry I haven't kept in touch better. It's just, after Ryan…"

Her face hardened. Sandra was not one for expressing her emotions out loud. "Yeah, I know. No worries."

Then because I was nothing if not irritating, I asked, "Did you process the scene?"

"For Conroy?" She cleared her throat and glanced down at her phone, sitting on her desk. "No, I had that day off. I was gambling at the casino." But the way she was evading my gaze made me think she was lying.

Maybe Marner was right—I had to move on. There was no end to the questions. There were no answers.

But what was I supposed to do about Detective Dead popping up in my house at will?

That was the five-thousand dollar question.

The next day, I was laying on my couch with a headache from the humidity and a long day of work when Ryan sat on my shins. Too tired to reprimand him, I just said "Hi," and continued to press a cold cloth to my forehead.

"Are you seriously dating Marner?" he asked by way of greeting.

I sighed. "I went out with him on something that could be called a coffee date. Why?"

"You do realize he's emotionally unavailable, don't you?"

"First of all, who are you, Dr. Phil? Second of all, I think you've mixed Jake up with yourself."

"Oh, we're calling him Jake now, are we?"

It felt strange, but I was. "Yes. We are."

"I wasn't kidding about the back hair. The guy is a gorilla. When we were at the beach he looked like an Asian sun bear. And Italians always cheat on their girlfriends."

My head pounded worse. "Is that based on empirical evidence or anecdotal?"

"I don't even know what that means, but it's true. Every Italian guy I know has stuck his fork in veal that wasn't his."

That was by far the weirdest description of infidelity I'd ever heard. "Has Marner cheated on his girlfriends?" I'd bet my fully renovated Victorian he hadn't.

"Well. No. But—"

Exactly. "That's all I need to know. Stop talking. I have a headache."

The air shifted and despite having closed my eyes I could sense him move closer to my upper body.

"Your phone is blowing up. You have a bunch of texts from Marner."

"Don't read those!" I sat up, grasping around the end table for my phone.

"Oh, and it looks like someone is threatening you."

That really made me panic. "What?"

It was an unknown number again.

Stay away from the station. Stay away from closed cases or you'll be dead.

Fear washed over me. "Oh my God, this is so creepy. How could someone know I was at the police station?"

"Because they're a cop." Ryan looked at me like that was the world's most obvious thing. "Who has your number?"

"Marner. DeAngelo. The girls in evidence." I sat all the way up. "It can't be any of them. And it's not Marner."

"So that leaves DeAngelo."

"But he doesn't know I'm investigating your death."

Ryan gave me a look of total skepticism. "Why, because you were so subtle?"

He had a point. Bailey Burke, crime writer, had not exactly been the world's greatest cover. "I never claimed to be a PI."

"He's texting again." Ryan gestured to my phone. "I think you should respond."

Apparently my safety was not priority number one to these guys. "That sounds dangerous."

"It says that you should meet him tonight at Edgewater Park."

I squeezed my damp washcloth so hard water dribbled onto my shirt. The somewhat see-through one I had worn to entice Marner. I swiped at it. "I'm not doing that. Only a complete idiot would do that."

"I'll go with you."

"You're a ghost, remember? You can't touch things."

"Then ask Marner to take you. But don't tell him why."

"He's not an idiot either. He never believes me when I lie or stretch the truth. He knows me too well."

Ryan shot me a long look. "How well does he know you?"

Oh hell no. "That's none of your business." Not as well as apparently Ryan was thinking.

"You can still go. Isn't Edgewater Live tonight? There will be a ton of people there listening to the free music at the beach."

"That's on Thursdays."

"So tell him you'll meet him tomorrow night. You can't be killed with two-thousand people there."

This was a bad idea. Yet I still found myself texting the unknown killer back.

Unfortunately, he said yes.

By the Proper Pig food truck. 7pm.

Almost immediately my phone rang. It was Sandra from evidence, which was weird. She hadn't called my cellphone in at least a year. "Hello?"

"Hey, it's Sandra." She was whispering. "Listen, you didn't hear this from me, and I'll deny it until the day I die, but DeAngelo made changes to the police report on Conroy's death. I saw two versions, totally by accident, because I may or may not have been having sex with DeAngelo on his desk at the time. There was a storm and the power went out that day and everyone left the station, and well…we lingered."

Shut the front door. Was literally everyone getting booty but me? It would seem so.

"Okay, so what was the discrepancy between the two?" I wasn't going to dwell on the Secret Sex Lives of Detectives.

"There were footprints in the snow—a woman's, given the shoe size—in the first report. Nothing in the second."

Very interesting. "Thanks, I appreciate you telling me."

"I don't know what it means, if anything, but I can't lie about stuff like that. It's bad karma." She gave a hurried goodbye and hung up on me.

I tossed my phone down and relayed everything she had told me to Ryan.

"I told you DeAngelo was shady."

It seemed he was right. "I still don't know what that means, in the grand scheme of things."

"That a woman killed me."

Which made no sense to me whatsoever. What woman would want Ryan dead, and how did he explain DeAngelo's involvement? My head continued to throb. "I need you to go away. If this is my last night on earth, I want to spend it peacefully." Because if

I was murdered, I had no doubt I would be stuck as Ryan's sidekick in the afterlife.

"You just want Marner to come over and feed you some Italian sausage."

I stuck my tongue out at Ryan. "You're disgusting." And possibly jealous, which I should not be so thrilled about, but I was.

"Remember the shoulder rug. That's all I'm saying."

I talked Alyssa into going to the park with me. Every Thursday night in summer, the city had a live band playing by the lakefront beach, with beer and food trucks. It was very casual, never overly crowded, yet a great place to catch the sunset and hear some music for free. There was a view of the downtown skyline and the beach, which, unlike in my childhood, was relatively clean. Not a needle in sight.

"I'm going to destroy a pulled pork sandwich," Alyssa said. She was wearing a bikini top that was struggling to contain her chest, and the cutest high-waisted polka dot shorts imaginable. Her hair was pulled back with a retro scarf. Men kept giving her and her cleavage appreciative glances.

I was covered in a long maxi dress, terrified my skin would spontaneously combust from exposure to the sun. I had already applied sunscreen twice and we had only been there seven minutes. I opened up my collapsible chair and warily scanned the crowd. There was a band playing whose enthusiasm far exceeded their skill. Really, sometimes you have to know not to touch the Beatles.

Since the dinner Alyssa wanted was from the very truck the person of interest had named as the meeting point, I went with her, scanning the area nervously. I hadn't told her anything, because I honestly didn't know what to say. I had started poking around doing research on the name of the man Ryan had received benefits for. I had also started digging to see who owned the LLC that disbursed the funds. But I had a job as well, and none of it was my area of expertise. I was stumbling around the Internet witlessly.

There was a guy standing in line in front of us who turned around and smiled. At me. "Bailey? It's Michael Kincaid, from high school. How are you? You look great."

I had a vague memory of the captain of the football team once nodding at me and asking to borrow a calculator in calculus, but we had never been friends. We hadn't even run in the same circles. I hadn't been a party girl. "Oh hi, Michael, wow. Good to see you."

"I heard you run your own business," he said, his teeth very white as he smiled. His eyes were shielded behind sunglasses but he was shirtless and in swim trunks, so I could see he hadn't lost his athleticism.

"Yes, it's small but I love it. You remember Alyssa?" I tilted my head. "She works with me sometimes but primarily she's an IT specialist."

"My, my, my, Michael Kincaid." Alyssa gave him a blinding smile. "You called me a heavyweight eater in the tenth grade."

His eyes widened. "What? I'm sorry, I don't even remember you."

"Of course you don't." Alyssa rolled her eyes. "Alyssa Dembowski. You and your crowd used to call me Alyssa Dem*cow*ski. I had brown hair then. Braces. I used to wear T-shirts that said things like "Think like a proton and stay positive.""

Understanding dawned on his face. "Oh, yeah, Alyssa…wow." He glanced down at her chest. "You've really grown up. You're…gorgeous."

Sometimes in the course of an ordinary life, you get restitution. Alyssa had just gotten hers. I knew without a doubt she'd be gloating over that until dark. "Thanks. You're not so bad yourself. But it was never your looks that were the issue."

The line moved up and Michael took a few steps backward toward the truck. He looked genuinely sheepish. "I'm really sorry for any and everything I ever said in high school. I was a show off and an idiot then. I'm much nicer now. Let me buy you a beer and make it up to you."

"Make it two and you've got yourself a deal."

While I sunk to third-wheel status, I realized this was the perfect opportunity to try to find Hostile Texter. I glanced at my phone. It was five to seven. "I'm not going to get a sandwich after all," I said, out of nowhere. "I need a minute to think about it."

Alyssa gave me a look like she thought I was insane for making such a random comment in the middle of her flirt session. Which I was. "Okay," she said.

I waved. "Good to see you, Michael."

Then I hovered around the barbecue sauce table, already regretting my decision to get out of line. That sauce smelled like heaven. No one looked suspicious or familiar. I went around the back of the truck, but I didn't see anything out of the ordinary. Circling back, I noticed Michael and Alyssa were gone.

"Hey," a guy said, nodding toward me. He was heavily tattooed and was wearing a pair of shorts drooping low on his hips, no shirt. He had on a baseball hat and he was approaching me fast.

I realized I was wedged between a truck and a trash can and I started to move, panicking a little.

But all he said was, "Do you have a lighter?"

Relief coursed through me. "No. I don't smoke."

I didn't. *Take that, Ryan Conroy.*

Since I didn't see anyone who looked as if they were trying to make eye contact with me, I decided to give in to the siren call of pulled pork and get back in line. It was now ten people deep, but I could hang tough for that barbecue sauce.

Moving back to where our chairs were set up, my sandwich cradled in my hands like a precious gem, I wondered where Ryan was. So much for his vow to protect me in the form of phantom police. Specter Security sucked.

He was sitting in my chair, leaning back with his eyes closed. "I heard that."

"What?"

"Specter Security sucks. That really hurts, Bai."

Alarm made my palms sweat. "I didn't say that out loud."

His eyes opened. "Really?" He looked impressed with himself. "Damn, I can read your mind now? That's next level."

"That's *awful*." My mind was a chaotic neurotic mess with thoughts of both him and Marner and lies and death and cravings for nicotine. "Stay out of my head."

"I didn't do it on purpose." He scanned the crowd. "This band sucks. And I would kill for a beer."

Because he was in my chair, I was forced to spread out my beach towel and sit down. I couldn't take Alyssa's seat without her thinking I was a loon. Besides, she would just unknowingly sit on Ryan and I had a feeling he would like that far too much. Sometimes it was hard to have a best friend who oozed sexuality while you leaked anxiety. For once, I wanted to be sexy.

"Oh God, stop," Ryan said. "Enough with the pity party. Is this because I said you're a tightass? I'm sorry. You have your hot moments too."

First of all, he was still in my head. Second of all, that was the worst attempt at reassurance I'd ever heard. "When have I ever had a hot moment? Don't patronize me, it's awkward for both of us."

"When we went to the Christmas party three years ago at work and you wore that navy-blue dress that barely covered your crotch. Your legs were a million miles long and you looked like you needed a guy to bend you over a—"

Ryan cut himself off. "Anyway, you were hot that night."

That made me warm. I had thought I looked good that night. I had felt confident in the bandage dress and those sky-high raspberry-colored heels. It was awesome to hear he had noticed. "Thanks. I appreciate it."

"That was before you lost too much weight."

And he ruined it.

"Get out of my chair."

He kicked sand at me with his boot. The amazing thing was it actually sprayed over my legs. Not a lot. But it happened. There was a pile of grains in the lap of my maxi dress. "Holy…"

"Oh yeah." Ryan fist pumped. "I'm getting stronger. This rocks."

It made me nervous. Not because I cared if he had the ability to move physical objects or not, but because it seemed to me that meant he was firmly entrenched in purgatory.

I was going to say something to that effect but then I realized a little girl a few feet away was staring at me. "Do you have an invisible friend too?" she asked.

Because of course I was talking to myself with everyone around me. Yikes. "Yes," I told her. "His name is Ryan."

She nodded, like this made total sense to her. "Mine's name is Bart. He died a long time ago. He whispers in my ear at night and it tickles."

Okay. Why were kids so eerie? "Does your mom know about Bart?"

"Yeah, but she doesn't believe me."

"I believe you."

She smiled and went back to slinging sand into a pail, the strap of her bathing suit sliding down her round shoulder. She was about five and she looked like a mini-me. Fair skin, red hair. She patted the sand with brutal efficiency and repeatedly brushed sand off her suit and legs when she got a dusting.

"This is why I am glad I never had kids," Ryan commented. "They're freaks."

Oddly, it was the first time I ever thought I might want some.

Chapter Eleven

THREATENING TEXTER WAS a no-show. All I learned from our night at the beach was that I can eat a full pound of pulled pork in one sitting, I might eventually want to reproduce, and Alyssa was going to revenge date Michael Kincaid. I also had a sunburned nose, despite my obsessive sunscreen application. Oh, and that Ryan could read my mind, which meant I was never safe from humiliation.

I decided on Friday that it was time to focus on my own business, instead of running around town in pursuit of phantom criminals. I had appointments the rest of the week, plus one with the Jensens the following Monday, which had surprised me. Usually after a home is staged clients have no further need for me until it's time to collect the rental furnishings, but Christy Jensen had said they wanted additional input, and since she was willing to pay for it, there was no reason to refuse.

Alyssa was with me in my home office, absorbed in her phone, gleeful that Michael had been texting her nonstop. "What an ass," she said. "I'm so going to string him along and dump him."

"Doesn't that seem mean?" I asked. "I mean, that was a long time ago. He was a dumb kid. Don't you want to be the mature one?"

"No." She started typing a response. "I was bullied mercilessly in high school, you know that. I was called fat basically every day, and Michael was the ringleader. They used to say, 'Rattle, rattle, here comes the cattle,' when I would walk into class."

Yeah, that was pretty bad. "Well then, I hope you get closure." I had been bullied for my freckles and for being a crybaby, but that was nothing compared to what Alyssa had endured. I think it was fair to say most of us had been bullied at one point or another, to varying degrees. "And that you don't get arrested for beating the crap out of him."

She laughed. "Trust me, I will keep it cool. After all, the best revenge is looking good."

My own phone buzzed. A text from Marner.

Call me.

For some reason, I found that intensely irritating. If he wanted to speak to me, why didn't he call *me*? Or actually text me whatever it was he wanted to discuss, since he'd taken the time to text a command. Also, a "How are you?" would have been a nice intro. It just sounded bossy. So after just lecturing Alyssa on maturity, I very childishly decided to ignore him.

I was busy, after all, and he had left me the other night with no idea what we were actually doing and then didn't say a word about it when he demanded I meet him at the station. And wait a minute. When I had left he had said "I'll call you later" and he hadn't. So the call burden was really on him.

"Random question," I said to Alyssa. "Do you think it's possible to help a ghost move on to the other side?" I had been up late thinking about Ryan. Worrying that he was stuck here indefinitely. That couldn't be healthy or fulfilling.

Alyssa burst out laughing. "That truly is the world's most random question."

"I'm serious. Do you think ghosts are trapped or do they have a purpose they have to achieve?" It made me think about my own mortality. What had I accomplished? Helping Ryan find peace would be way more important than figuring out why I couldn't seem to drink alcohol without winding up on the floor.

"I don't know. I think that if that's the case, I hope they make it clear, or I'm going to be wandering around indefinitely. I have no clue what my higher purpose would be."

"Me either." It made me want to eat a burger. "Want to go get lunch? Philosophizing makes me hungry."

"Everything makes me hungry." Alyssa stretched. "Is it wrong to sleep with Michael Kincaid even though I have no intention of dating him?"

"I'm not here to judge." Personally, I couldn't imagine doing that. I had never been able to separate sex from emotion. Part of me envied her though, because Alyssa walked around owning her choices. I second-guessed everything. "But what if you end up falling for him?"

"I highly doubt that."

"I don't know. I think you might be playing with fire. Just be careful."

Alyssa scoffed. "When have you ever known me to be careful? I'm not going to start now."

That made me laugh. "True."

"How about Mexican for lunch? Since you're going to Rocky River, let's hit Barrio. It's on the way."

"Sounds good." Now that my appetite had returned, I might as well be a glutton. Besides, Barrio had build your own tacos and a hot sauce wall that was free for customer use. I may not be hot-hot, but I do like spice in my food. The restaurant had a Dia de los Muertos theme with cool sugar skull artwork on the walls. My appetite was definitely back as I attacked a taco trio.

We were debating ordering a second round of guacamole when I got another text from Marner.

DeAngelo is dead.

I dropped my phone like it was on fire. "Oh my God!" I said to Alyssa. "DeAngelo died." I quickly texted Marner back, asking him what had happened.

"Who is DeAngelo?" Alyssa asked. "Should we be sad or relieved?"

I willed Marner to respond, but nothing. I took a sip of my water, wanting to rid myself of the sudden lump in my throat. "Not relieved. Sad. I mean, DeAngelo's the kind of guy who makes you mildly uncomfortable with his constant flirting, but I don't think he was a bad person." I did wonder though about Ryan's concerns. And about the texts I had gotten from an unknown number. The no-show texter at the park. Had it all been DeAngelo?

"Was he a cop?"

"Yes. Sorry."

"Did he get killed on duty?" Alyssa picked up her phone and starting tapping. "I'm looking it up."

I hadn't thought of that. If he had been killed on duty, it would be on the news. Marner still wasn't responding.

"Detective found dead in his home last night by his girlfriend," Alyssa read off her phone. "Cause of death undetermined, though he was a known diabetic."

"That's weird." I shoved a chip in my mouth, needing to chew on something crunchy. "What does that mean? If he was killed, they would say that, right?"

"I don't know. They don't usually like to declare something a murder right away, do they? They have to eliminate other possibilities." Alyssa put her phone down. "Ask Marner about it."

"I did. He's not answering me." It was a very Marner thing to do. Reel me in, then leave me dangling.

"I feel guilty," I told Alyssa. "I found DeAngelo annoying. Plus I thought he was probably involved in some sketchy things." He couldn't be Ryan's killer though, if he himself had been killed. But wait, I was leaping to conclusions. He might have had a heart attack or choked on an olive or gone into insulin shock. I couldn't get Sandra's words out of my head though. DeAngelo had falsified police reports. He had stolen money from a drug bust. He knew Ryan had made a will. Was he somehow involved in the investments Ryan kept referring to?

"It's okay to not like someone when they were alive but still feel bad they died. It's not like you wished him dead—you don't have to feel guilty over not liking him."

I still did though. I couldn't help it. I had entertained DeAngelo as a legitimate suspect in Ryan's death, and now I wasn't sure what a mysterious, "undetermined" death meant. "Do you think I should go to the funeral?"

"Did you sleep with him?" Alyssa asked, polishing off her margarita.

"What?" The thought made my skin crawl. "Of course not!"

"Then you don't have to go to his funeral."

"I doubt that's an official rule of etiquette." It would certainly explain the crowd of women at Ryan's funeral though.

"It's just my personal code of conduct. Physical intimacy requires I be present when they're dropped in the ground. It keeps me from sleeping around."

"Then you better hope Michael Kincaid doesn't drop dead or you'll need a black dress."

Alyssa just laughed. "True that."

Suddenly, I wondered what I would do if something happened to Marner. He was a cop after all, and at risk every day.

But I didn't want to go there, so I hailed the waiter and ordered more guac, determined to eat my feelings rather than confront them.

My phone buzzed. I rushed to look at it, hoping it was a text from Marner.

Fear crawled up my spine. It was from *DeAngelo*. I had saved his number in my contacts when he'd texted me the first time as Dirty DeAngelo.

There was no threat. No explanation. It was a simple kiss emoji, accompanied by a wink. A kiss and a wink from DeAngelo on a Friday didn't seem that odd.

Except that DeAngelo was dead, found the night before by his girlfriend.

And while the dead could rise, they couldn't text.

Or could they?

I drained my margarita and tried not to have a panic attack.

Sometimes your mother warns you not to do something and you do it anyway. Like when I was fifteen and decided I wanted to be goth and dyed my hair black. She told me I would look like a vampire, and not a sparkly one, and she was right. It took an entire year and hundreds of dollars in salon visits to gradually match my hair to the new growth. Plus, I sported Emma Watson's pixiecut for most of tenth grade. Bad, really bad, idea.

Going to DeAngelo's apartment alone? Possibly even a worse idea.

I don't know what I was expecting to find, but I knew one thing for sure—he wouldn't be there. He was dead, and the thought had been weighing on me for the last twenty-four hours. I kept thinking that maybe, just maybe, I could call on DeAngelo's ghost to explain to me what the hell was going on. It seemed like he was right in the thick of all of this, and if I could see Ryan, who was to say I couldn't see DeAngelo if he were trapped in his apartment where he died?

It was a stretch. Ryan said he had chosen me as his contact, but what about ghosts that appeared to wander with no purpose? People talked about that phenomena all the time. I had to do something, and it was either this or crawl out of my skin, and I kind of like my skin, despite the soft dusting of freckles.

So I found myself standing outside of DeAngelo's condo, which I had found by doing a property search, wondering how I thought I was going to get inside. It was in a low-slung sixties-built building and the hallway was gloomy and quiet. I didn't see any surveillance cameras anywhere. I also didn't see anywhere that a spare key would be tucked. No doormat, no potted plants in a hallway like this. No mailbox. Damn it.

I decided to just try the knob. To my shock, it turned easily and yawned open at a soft push. Glancing guiltily down the hall, I stepped inside and shut the door behind me. It was hushed in the apartment, and gloomy, despite the blinds being open. The windows were high and squat and the balcony railing was actually a concrete wall, which further blocked the sun. There was no evidence of any sort of struggle or anything suspicious. It was a tidy apartment, although a quick glance around showed a few candy wrappers next to the couch. My heart was hammering in my chest. Marner was going to kill me if he knew I was here.

Ryan might back me up, but I didn't want to talk to him. I wanted to talk to DeAngelo.

"Hey, DeAngelo, it's Bailey Burke," I whispered in the empty living room. I felt ridiculous, and a little terrified. Of what, I wasn't sure. "Can you talk to me? Can you tell me what happened? If you talk, I'll be able to hear you, I promise." I thought I would be able to hear him, anyway. It wasn't a guarantee.

Nothing. DeAngelo didn't walk around a corner and give me a smarmy grin. I was torn being disappointment and relief. I was used to Ryan's ghost. The freak factor might be high with a second spirit. I wandered around, not sure what the heck I was looking for. Anything suspicious would have been taken by the cops, and they didn't have it cordoned off as a crime scene, clearly. But I also knew that whoever had texted me from DeAngelo's phone had to be someone who had access to the scene. So it could be DeAngelo's girlfriend, which seemed ridiculous. The EMTs. Or a cop. The last option made me shiver despite the heat of the stuffy apartment.

In the kitchen there was an empty orange juice container on the counter, given credence to the theory that DeAngelo went into diabetic shock. Between the juice and the candies, he must have been trying to regulate his sugar levels.

I peeked in the fridge, using my sweater sleeve to open the door, expecting to see his insulin kit, but it wasn't on the mostly bare shelves.

Then a blow to the head sent me reeling into darkness.

When I woke up, the room was spinning, the cool air of the fridge wafting over me. I gave a groan and sat up, my stomach rebelling. I swallowed back a gag and hauled myself to my knees. Someone had hit me and I needed to get the heck out of Dodge. I used the refrigerator shelves to help right myself, and that was when I realized that in a previously blank spot sat an insulin kit.

It hadn't been there before. I was sure of it.

Which meant DeAngelo had been murdered by a clever killer who had stolen his insulin.

But no one was going to believe me.

parl=

The question was why. What did DeAngelo know?

I thought about the money. The investment account Ryan had mentioned. They always say follow the money and you'll find the killer.

All I needed was to do that before the killer decided they were tired of warning me and made me their next victim.

Chapter Twelve

"NO ONE IS being truthful with me," I told Ryan, frustrated. It was Sunday and he was lying on my couch watching football. "Chill out."

"Someone hit me," I reminded him. "I'm in danger." I had gotten myself home from DeAngelo's, then had spent the night checking my locks over and over. I had finally called and set up an appointment for the following week to install a home security system.

"If they wanted to kill you, they would have. They just wanted to knock you out for a minute." He gave a yell as a man in tight pants leaped into the air.

I was too frazzled to even comprehend who was playing. "That's reassuring, thanks. I feel so much better now."

"Good."

"What are we missing?" It kept going around and around in my head that this was about money, not drugs. "Tell me about the five grand, Ryan."

"Don't worry about it."

I stared at him for a minute, but he wasn't even looking at me. I threw my hands up in the air and told him, "I'm seriously going to give up here. I want out. None of this is my problem, and no one is telling me what I need to know."

Ryan finally deigned to look at me. "Bai, you need to back off. It's cool. Leave this to the cops to sort out."

Why was that not even remotely reassuring? Uneasy, I tried to figure out this new angle. But I didn't know what to think. I didn't even really know Ryan. Not truly. "Just like that?" I asked.

"Yeah. I think it's better if you just ease up." He rubbed his chin. "I couldn't live with myself if something happened to you."

"But you're dead," I joked, needing to find some humor. Ryan being serious was more unnerving than anything else up to this point.

"Yeah, and I want to be the only one who is."

It would give me warm fuzzies if I weren't shivering from the idea of dying. Back off. I could do that. Done. Backed all the way up. Like a big old truck.

Monday, I went over to the Jensens and greeted Christy with a smile when she opened the door, determined to put life back to normal. "Hi, how are you? How has traffic been with the showings?"

"I think we're overpriced." She winked. "Don't tell Tim. He thinks the problem is that he didn't listen to you about his office. He's in there now and would like to finally be reasonable and clean out the clutter. Like maybe disassemble his rifle collection." Behind her hand she murmured, "Don't let him do too much, though, if you know what I mean. I'm still not moving."

Great. I was being pulled into their marital dispute over moving. "Hmm," I said. "That sounds tricky. I'm not sure how to walk that fine line."

Christy just laughed. "Honey, just make him think he's getting what he wants. Didn't we talk about this before?"

Feeling monstrously uncomfortable, I glanced down at my phone when it buzzed.

Call me NOW.

Marner was getting sassy. I had texted him an hour ago and

he hadn't replied and now he was making demands? I was about to tell him to cool his jets but then he texted again.

Found out who owns the investment company. Someone named Tim Jensen, and his brother is one of our IT guys. Looks like the Peppers guy is a made up account/name. Turns out IA is already onto it. Been investigating. DeAngelo might have been onto it.

I stopped walking. What the hell? *The* Tim Jensen? The same Tim Jensen whose house I was in? Well, so much for backing out of this whole situation.

Christy had told me her husband owned an insurance and investment firm. But it was just a coincidence too huge to be real. Unless it *wasn't* a coincidence.

Wait a minute… Officer Jensen. His first name was Caleb. Caleb Jensen. At the open house for Ryan's listing. He had been there, and I hadn't thought jack about it. I mentally kicked myself from here to Tuesday.

Tim was in his cluttered office, the walls loaded down with books and animal trophies and rifles. I looked at his gun closet in a whole new light. He was potentially a thief with a whole lot of weaponry. Yet I still couldn't believe what Marner had found meant anything other than the possibility that he was helping cops with their retirement accounts. "Hi, Tim, how are you?"

He didn't smile. "Annoyed. This house should have sold. I think I need to take your advice and clear out everything personal in this office."

"Sure, no problem." I had initially liked this couple, but now they just seemed indulgent and entitled. Spurred on by that feeling and the realization that he had done work for the department, or at least some of the staff, I said, "So I just figured out your brother works for the police department. I knew there was an Officer Jensen, but I didn't realize he was your brother."

Tim stayed in his chair behind his desk and stared at me. "He's my half-brother actually. My father had a mid-life crisis. Caleb is fifteen years younger than me."

That got me exactly nowhere. "What an interesting family." I wasn't sure what else to say.

"You could say that. Caleb is also a little shady. I think the term is "dirty cop.""

Now I was really off-kilter. Why would he tell me that? I just gave him a noncommittal smile.

Tim stood up. "So what do I do about everything on the desk and the walls? Can you pack it up for me?"

"Of course. I have boxes in the car."

"Christy will go get them. Give her your keys."

That seemed odd. But Tim seemed like an odd guy and he had been the same the first time I'd met him. "I can do it."

"No, Christy needs something to do with herself. She's bored." He gave his wife a weird smile.

Christy narrowed her eyes. The tension grew and it was awkward as hell.

I decided to quickly text Marner back.

Tim Jensen is one of my clients. I'm at his house now.

"What should I do with this?" Tim asked, gesturing to photos spread out in front of him.

This was definitely a client who needed me to pick up everything and file it away myself. He was not going to lift a finger. When I came around the desk, I shoved my phone in my pocket, and stared down at the piles of papers he had. I stopped cold. "What—"

I couldn't finish the sentence, words eluding me.

On the desk was a photo. A crime scene photo. Ryan's car. The park. I thought for a minute that I was going to faint. The room spun and dizziness threatened to pull me under. It was taken from outside the vehicle and there was a police car in the bottom left corner, just a portion of it. The car looked forlorn in the bleak landscape of a winter woodland setting. There was blood all over the window. Everywhere. It was like someone had taken a bucket of paint and thrown it on the glass.

"Why do you have that?" I whispered, swallowing over and over, trying to hold down the nausea. I wanted to vomit.

This was what Marner had refused to show me. With good reason. It was stark and real and horrible. That was *Ryan*.

"My brother gave it to me. So that I could show you." His

long fingers reached out and picked up the photograph. "It's a suicide, you can see that. Right?" He shoved the picture close to my face.

Ryan's blood was eye level with me. "What are you doing? What's going on?" My phone was buzzing in my pocket but I only registered that somewhere in the back of my mind. My focus was on the hypnotizing view of what had happened to my friend's life. To his head. Oh geez, I gripped the edge of the desk.

"I'm making sure you realize that no one is going to listen to you. A scrawny redheaded home stager, of all things, who is pining for her dead friend, who was a drug user, a lover of hookers, and a loose cannon. My brother says everyone knows Conroy was impulsive, and no one was surprised when he bit it."

I am, generally speaking, not slow on the uptake, but this was taking me more than a minute. I was both shocked to realize that Tim was in some way, somehow, involved in Ryan's death, and seriously ticked off that I had never made the connection. Plus, I had staged his stupid, pretentious house for no apparent reason. He was most likely never intending to sell it. Dumbfounded, I actually said that out loud. "You never wanted me to stage your house?"

Tim frowned. "What? Of course I did. Why else would I call you? I mean, we're not actually worried about you being able to point fingers. I just thought you'd like to see what *really* happened."

He was making me sick from showing me these images purely for his own sadistic pleasure. I wanted to punch him in the nose or knee him in the nutsack.

Except for one little fact. The man was surrounded by guns. Including one on his desk, even though he wasn't holding it or even reaching for it.

"I don't know what any of this has to do with you," I managed to say.

"You're lying." Tim shook his head like he was insulted that I would try that tactic. "You've been nosing around, going to the police station, asking questions. Looking pathetic."

Mr. Charming. If he wanted me to go away quietly, insulting

me wasn't the way to do it. But I didn't think he wanted me to go away quietly. *Think, Bailey, you're not an idiot.* My pockets were roomy and I slipped my hands into them, trying to turn my phone on record from spatial memory. It was about a one in ten chance that I was going to be able to achieve an active recording, but I had to try. "I don't think Ryan killed himself. I knew him well."

Yet in the corner of my mind it niggled at me that maybe I didn't know Ryan all that well. I'd had that very thought the day before.

"Funny though, that he never once mentioned you, according to Caleb. It wasn't until much later that I realized you were hung up on him, after Christy told me about your little chat about ghosts. Hiring you really was a coincidence. My friend Bill used you to stage his condo. But anyway I can assure you, Ryan wasn't hung up on you, according to my brother."

Now he was just trying to rattle me. "Why would Ryan talk to his co-worker about a friend? That's just stupid. Why does it matter anyway?"

"Because of you, and that other detective's crush on you, shit is getting stirred up that wasn't supposed to be stirred up. Connections made, questions asked. Now your friend knows that I'm the one who's committing fraud, stealing from the pensions of the guys' using my services, while my brother creates false patrolmen and other staff members." He gestured with his hands. "Classic shell game. Look over here while I do something over there. But I know the the cops are on to us, and in this case, my brother is going to have to take the fall. I am going to throw him under the proverbial bus."

Pieces fell into place. I was furious I had been so dumb. Why did people commit crimes? Money, revenge, jealousy. Very rarely anything else. I should have followed the money from the beginning. "So why am I here?" I was pretty sure I knew why, but I needed to hear it said out loud before I completely and totally lost my cool.

"Because I wanted my house staged. And I thought you deserved to know the truth."

"But I'm not going to prison for murder." A female voice came from behind me.

Shut the front door. I hadn't seen that one coming either. I swiveled around to see Christy standing in the doorway pointing a gun at me. What. The. Hell. She was wearing a blouse, for crying out loud. She had children, who I sincerely hoped were at daycare or summer camp. School hadn't started yet. She seemed normal. I had confided in her. Oh crap, I had told her Ryan was a ghost. They must have thought I was coming unhinged or something. Well, that made three of us.

Tim swore. "Christy, knock it off." He sounded more annoyed than anything.

I wasn't sure what the heck was going on, but I had to ask. "So you killed Ryan?" I asked. My voice trembled, but I got the words out. My palms were sweating and I wanted to throw up. "Tim wasn't there?"

"Of course not. Do you think a cop was going to go to a secluded location with Tim? Hardly." She used her left hand to gesture to her chest. "On the other hand, I'm *very* persuasive. Plus Ryan was swallowing Vicodin like nobody's business that day."

Equally as charming as her husband, with her callous disregard for Ryan's life. "So you murdered an innocent man over money? A few thousand dollars? That makes you a vile human being." The horror and reality of the situation had fallen over me. I was going to die unless I did something immediately, and I was no savvy chick. If Ryan hadn't been able to protect himself, how could I?

"It's actually more like half a million dollars, really, over the last three years. But we never meant for it to get so out of hand, and truthfully, your friend was suicidal. He felt guilty over popping pills and the fact that he was cheating on his girlfriend with me."

"Total lie," Ryan said behind me. "I never cheated on Hannah."

I was grateful for his presence, but I wasn't sure it was going to do me any good in this circumstance. He was powerless without a body.

"And technically, he did pull the trigger. It's easy to be suggestive with someone who is high as a kite."

I couldn't hear this. I didn't want to know or picture those horrible, senseless final moments for Ryan. I turned to Tim, wanting to appeal to whatever compassion he had. He was pointing a gun at me as well.

"If you're going to shoot me, just do it," I told Tim. "I don't need to hear your ridiculous justifications or your gloating."

"No one is going to shoot you."

"I wouldn't be so sure of that," Christy said.

It was then I realized that Tim wasn't only pointing the gun at me, he was watching his wife carefully. I started to think maybe she was the more dangerous of the two.

"This is fun," she added. "You probably thought it was some huge conspiracy, like a mob hit, or drug dealers, or a pimp. And yet it was just so simple. Just a dirty cop."

From somewhere deep inside me, the anger that these idiots, these self-important jerks, had been behind the murder of Ryan, boiled over and made me bold enough to say, "Blah, blah, blah. You just love to hear yourself talk, don't you?"

Tim actually laughed. "True. So you have met my wife."

Christy's face twisted into an expression of fury. "This isn't funny."

It wasn't, but that fact became more real and urgent when Tim came around the desk. I hadn't thought he was the one to worry about. He grabbed my wrist. Hard. I can say with all honestly that before this, I'd never been aware of being in danger. Even when I got knocked out at DeAngelo's, I hadn't known it was coming. There had been no time for fear. Once I had skidded on the highway during a snowstorm and hit the railing before sputtering to a stop, unharmed, but to this point it had been the scariest moment of my life. I didn't know what to do with this, which was equally dangerous and not looking to be over in the blink of an eye. It was so terrifying it almost felt improbable. As ridiculous as Ryan being a ghost. Yet there he was, cursing behind me like an angry sailor. And I was going to die.

"No, it's not funny," I told Tim. "But what I don't understand is why you felt the need to drag me into this in the first place. I never would have figured this out on my own."

"Crazy people do crazy things." Tim gave me a smile. "How's that for your philosophical nugget of the day?"

Not exactly anything I was going to stitch on a sampler. "What now?"

"You are going to die of smoke inhalation when I burn this house to the ground," Christy said.

Didn't see that one coming either. "Uh…"

"This is bullshit," Ryan said. "There is no way that I was killed by these idiots. I must have done myself in to get away from all the stupid."

Wait, so now while I was facing death, he was going to claim suicide? It seemed a little irrelevant at the moment.

And the Jensen's plan was idiotic. If it were me, I'd make it look like my home stager had accidentally shot herself packing up guns, not realizing one was loaded.

"Are you just going to go along with this?" I asked Tim, trying to appeal to his sense of justice. He might be a greedy thief, but was probably not a murderer.

"I choose my battles with Christy," was all he said, giving me a shrug.

Nice. "Why would I be dead in your house while no one else is here? How are you going to explain arson? The fire investigators will know. This house is huge. In the amount of time it would take to trap me behind flames, I could have escaped ten times. I mean, presumably you have smoke detectors. Also, I would never commit suicide in a stranger's house. That's just *dumb*." It was. I figured it was worth it to point out the severe flaws in their plan before they carried it out. Maybe it would cause them to hesitate and I could figure out an escape.

Or it might make them just shoot me. Either way, I had to take a chance, and you know, sometimes you just had to make people aware they were lunatics.

"She's right," Christy said.

"For a smart man, you haven't really thought this through."

He hadn't. I was both surprised and relieved. "But then again, Christy admitted to me she's no rocket scientist."

I was being too mouthy, but I figured I had to go down with a fight. I wasn't going to talk a lunatic into anything, and Christy liked to think she was so persuasive. Let her see I knew full well she was more beauty than brains.

"Bailey, you need to shut up," Ryan said.

Since he wasn't giving me any solutions, I resented that. "What do you want me to do?" I demanded.

But Tim thought I was talking to him. "Take a bullet then, like your buddy did." And then he aimed a gun right at me. "Or duck."

Right then, without warning, Ryan came at Tim. Where I would have expected his body to just pass through Tim's, he actually managed to shove the gun. He had found his ability to move an object. Holy moly. Tim stumbled, the gun pointing downward. I took the opportunity to grab a stapler off the desk and hurl it at him.

Spinning, I also snagged a taxidermied animal off an end table, intending to smack Christy in the pie hole with it. But she was gone. She was running down the hallway to her kitchen. I had no idea why, nor did I give a damn. I headed for the front door just as a shot rang out. I screamed and ducked, but the bullet went through the open office door and I had already turned right. I threw open the front door and went careening down the steps onto the grass and almost choked on my relief when I saw a squad car pulling into the driveway. I had no idea why they were there, but I was going to launch myself behind their protection.

Officers stepped out, one detaining me, while the other proceeded into the house. I was babbling, trying to explain that I was in danger, when Marner pulled into the drive behind him. He got out and jogged over, telling the officer, "I've got this. Call for backup."

"He has a gun in there!" I shrieked at all of them, just to make sure they weren't running into a psycho insurance man ambush.

"What the hell is going on?" Marner demanded, running his eyes over me.

"Tim shot at me. Or actually, maybe it was Christy. I don't know!" I wanted to burst into tears but I bit my lip hard so I wouldn't give in.

Marner swore. "I'll kill that guy."

"How did you know to come here?" He was dragging me over to his car, and I let him, wanting away from that house of horrors. I briefly wondered where Ryan was, but I figured they couldn't hurt him anyway.

"You called me. That was a great idea. I couldn't hear everything, it was too muffled. But I knew something was wrong and you had already texted me you were here." Marner opened the passenger door to his car and helped me in. "That guy has stolen a freaking massive amount of money. Internal Affairs contacted the FBI weeks ago. This is their territory. Wait here."

He had his gun out of his holster and he went toward the house. I resisted the urge to scream and prevent him from doing his job. Instead I leaned back and attempted to release my shoulders from their position up near my ears. I was still holding the dead animal Tim had had stuffed. Glancing down into my lap I felt my stomach rebel at the view of the former living creature staring up at me with glass eyes. Just the icing on the bizarre cake.

Ryan appeared next to me. "Nice otter."

"Is that what this is?" I tossed it in the back seat. "Yuck. Thanks for saving me."

"Mostly you saved yourself, but I'm glad I could help." Ryan closed his eyes briefly then gave me an agonized glance. "I screwed up my life, didn't I?"

I was still reeling from my near-death experience so I didn't sugarcoat it. "I think you did make some questionable choices."

"I was letting him pay me to keep quiet about the money. I had found out the week before totally by accident." Ryan rubbed his chin. "I'm not a nice guy, you know that?"

That made my heart hurt. "I think you're a guy who has known a lot of love, and not a lot of hardship. You let yourself get a little greedy. Sadly, in the end, the only one it hurt was you. So there's no point in beating yourself up now."

"Marner wouldn't have done that. He would have blown the whistle."

I stayed silent because I thought there was a high probability of that being true.

It didn't matter anyway, because Ryan disappeared when Marner returned and got in the car. His jaw worked as he looked at me.

"Is everything okay?"

"Yeah. The wife shot the husband. Clipped him on the arm when she doubled back around and aimed through the garden window."

"Seriously?" My jaw dropped. "They're both nuts!"

"Yep. Nutty as fruitcakes. The scene is secure, but I need to take you down to the station for questioning."

"Okay." I gestured to the backseat, needing a moment of levity. "What about the otter?"

Marner glanced behind him and swore. "That's messed up." He gripped the steering wheel after he started the car but he didn't drive.

"Are you okay?" I wasn't sure if he was upset about the shady dealings Ryan had been involved in, or something else.

"Jesus, Bailey, that scared the hell out of me. I thought…"

"Thought what?"

"That something was going to happen to you."

I swallowed. "Me too."

He tapped his forearm, where his Celtic cross tattoo was. "This tat is for Ryan. Don't make me have to ink another cross on the other arm."

My throat tightened. That touched me. "I don't want to be a cross on your arm either. Thanks for being there."

"Yeah. No problem." But he wasn't looking at me. The mask was back in place. He had retreated and I had the sinking feeling that this might be the end of me and Marner before we'd ever even truly gotten started.

I searched for some levity, a way to reach him, make him less dour. "I wonder if I can still bill Tim and Christy for the last hour?"

"Not funny."

But it kind of was. "What happened to DeAngelo?" I asked, wondering if his death was at all related to this.

"Complications from diabetes. His girlfriend said his insulin was missing."

I shuddered, images of DeAngelo searching desperately in the fridge for the insulin that should have been there flashing through my head. "That's not funny at all."

"Nope."

I wanted to say something profound, or to express to Marner how I felt about him, given the fragility of life. But my emotions were too jumbled. I settled for, "I'll go to the funeral with you, okay?"

Marner didn't speak. But his hand left the wheel and found mine. He held it tightly for the whole drive.

Chapter Thirteen

M ARNER ASKED ME if I wanted my parents to pick me up after questioning, but I couldn't deal with my mother. Somehow, she would passive-aggressively suggest that I was at fault for nearly getting myself killed. Instead, I took an Uber, with a stop at the liquor store, and invited Alyssa over, but she was on a date with Michael. She offered to ditch him but I told her not to. I felt fine, just…weird. Not like before, when I was being compressed by grief. It was more restlessness than depression. Like this should be the ending, but it was more of a beginning than anything else.

I pulled up a show on my DVR that was light and fluffy. A cupcake competition, complete with burned batter, runny butter-cream and tears. I kept looking at my phone, thinking, hoping, Jake would text me, but he didn't.

Pulling a blanket over myself, despite the fact that it was ninety degrees outside, I popped my feet out from under the bottom and stared at my toes. The polish was chipped. When had that happened?

Ryan sat down next to me. "Hey."

"Hey."

We stayed silent beyond that, and after a minute I stood up. "Remember how you always wanted people to do a shot of Jameson at your funeral? A ton of people did, but I couldn't. My throat felt closed." I padded over to my kitchen. "But I bought a bottle of whiskey today." I turned. "Today I'm taking a shot for you. For your life. For our friendship."

He looked touched. "That's pretty awesome. I appreciate that."

"The timing seems better." I had shot glasses, though I wasn't sure why. They must have been remnants of my days wanting to fit in in college before I realized I was never going to be able to drink like a fish. I pulled two shooters down from the cabinet and opened the bottle and poured a finger in each. I knew Ryan couldn't drink it, but it seemed the polite thing to do.

"Sláinte," I said, and raised my glass. I had grown up with the Irish toast to good health on everyone's lips and so had Ryan.

He said it as well as I shuddered from the burn pouring down my throat.

"Sláinte. Now you have to take the second shot."

I gave a little cough and pounded my chest. I had almost died at the hands of an insurance agent, of all ridiculous things. I could deal with the whiskey. "You got it."

"Here's to women's kisses, and to whiskey, amber clear; not as sweet as a woman's kiss, but a darn sight more sincere."

"I've never kissed anyone insincerely," I told him wryly.

Ryan gave a snort. "I'll have to ask Marner."

He had to bring that up. I tossed this shot back readily. I didn't want to discuss Marner with him. I set the glass down on the countertop and looked at Ryan.

In that moment, it occurred to me that this might be it—the last time I would see him. He was going to get his one-way ticket to that bounce house in the sky and this time, it would be for real. I would never see him again. He seemed to realize that too. He actually was surprisingly somber for Ryan.

"Thanks, Bai. I mean that. I couldn't have done this without you." He tried to draw me into his arms, but of course I couldn't press on him or feel his touch.

I pretended I could. I leaned to an approximation of where his chest would be and looked up the length of his body to his face. His expression so rare for him, yet his face so familiar. I hoped that he had found peace. Hell, I hoped I had. "You're welcome. I've always loved you, Ryan." There, I said it. Not in a romantic kind of love way, but as the platonic love that it had always been, even when I hadn't understood that.

It was said with no expectation of him saying anything in return. He wasn't sentimental. But he surprised me. His voice was gruff, but he managed, "I love you too."

Then I think we were both waiting for him to get sucked away. The air seemed to be suspended around us and I could have sworn I heard the whistle of a train way in the distance. Coming to get him? But then again, I live in a fairly urban neighborhood. We do have a train. So it probably wasn't the Ethereal Express coming to give Ryan a ride to the afterlife.

The moment went on and on and moved from comforting and melancholy to anticipatory, and then just plain awkward. I took a step back. Our celestial hug had gone on too long.

"What the hell?" Ryan asked when the silence was deafening. "Now what?"

"I don't know. Did you pass your exam?" I had forgotten about that. His Intro to Death class had been giving him hell. No pun intended.

"I mean, barely, but I passed." He looked around. "Is there a waiting period or something? Do I have to be quarantined until I'm cleared by customs?"

If I was a betting woman, I'd put up my house against the fact that Ryan had missed something in the manual somewhere. He was a skimmer.

My e-cigarette was in the spice cabinet. I know, a poor attempt at camouflage. It wasn't like lingering among the curry and the Old Bay was going to prevent me from smoking it. I pulled it down and pushed the little button and took a hit. I justified it by the fact that it had been three days since I'd used it, and I had faced down the barrel of a gun.

"If you hadn't almost been killed today I would reprimand you. But I won't."

"Wow, thanks, that wasn't passive-aggressive at all."

We looked at each other and started laughing. I poured myself another shot. Last one, pinky swear.

Ten minutes later Ryan was lying on my couch like he was in therapy and I was drunk. "Why am I still here?" he asked.

If that wasn't the burning question I didn't now what was. "I don't know. Why are any of us here?"

I was in my big overstuffed chair, puffing away and feeling very warm in my extremities.

He gave me a look. "Thanks, Socrates."

"The only thing I know is that I know nothing," I said, pulling a true Socratic quote from the depths of my whiskey-soaked brain. "I thought you said once we solved your murder you would get to cross over." And he was still here, showing up at random intervals and criticizing my flat butt.

"I may have miscalculated."

"Are you okay?" I asked him. "With the way everything went down?" I didn't want him to wander around indefinitely with regret and guilt.

"Yeah. It is what it is. My own fault." He rolled onto his side and propped his head up with his hand. "Just tell my mom that I love her, okay? That she did right by me."

"She knows that."

His nose twitched. "Yeah."

We were a couple of sad sacks, that was for sure. "Have you gotten a text or anything?" I asked. "You know, from the Office of Purgatory?" I felt ridiculous saying that out loud.

"Nope. They're icing me out. Bastards."

"I'm not sure I would mess with them if you want to get a pass to heaven."

"Hmm." He started doing stomach crunches. "I wonder if I should keep up my workout regimen."

Obviously he was very concerned about his future (not.) "I'm hungry. I wonder if I have any cheese." Chips didn't usually tempt me, but dairy was my soul mate. The whiskey had me feeling relaxed, warm.

The minute I stepped into the kitchen that disappeared instantly.

A scream caught in the back of my throat and my heart jumped into high gear. My buzz instantly wore off as I took in the sight of Hannah, Ryan's paramour, sitting at my kitchen table. "How did you get in here?" I asked, glancing to the back door. Still locked.

Oh hell no…

She was trying to touch an orange piled high in my fruit bowl. Her finger kept going through it. Slowly she turned and looked at me. Her jaw worked but she didn't speak. There was terror in her eyes, and her mascara was staining her cheeks in angry black streaks.

"Uh, Ryan, can you come in here, please?" I called out, frozen in place. I was actually afraid to spook the spook. She didn't seem to know where she was and her face displayed no recognition of me.

"Is this where you flash me?" he responded. "I'm telling Marner."

"Just get in here!"

He groaned but he peeled himself off the couch and came toward the kitchen. "What… Hannah? Hey. What are you doing here? God, it's good to see you."

He was going to go to her, that was obvious, but I stepped in front of him and gave him a warning look. "Ryan," I whispered urgently. "Hannah's dead."

He stopped in his tracks and his eyes widened. "For real?" He peered around my head like if he moved too fast she would evaporate. "Oh crap. That's a problem."

"What is going on here?" I asked.

"Help me," Hannah said, her voice plaintive and frightened, completely at odds with the confident street-smart woman I had met. "He's after me."

"Ryan, you need to pull out your death manual, because I think we might have just found your next task."

Though why she was sitting in *my* house I had no answer. One ghost was managable. Two was a crowd.

My status as third wheel was firmly entrenched.

Ryan went to comfort Hannah.

I went for the hunk of mozzarella tempting me from my fridge.

Then poured the rest of the whiskey down the sink and braced myself for what appeared to be my new reality—counselor to the recently departed.

From home stager to BGG—Best Ghost Girlfriend. That's me.

Also by Erin McCarthy

Want to read more of Bailey's ghostly adventures in crime solving?

MURDER BY DESIGN SERIES

GONE WITH THE GHOST

SILENCE OF THE GHOST

ONCE UPON A GHOST

HOW THE GHOST STOLE CHRISTMAS (holiday novella)

IT'S A GHOST'S LIFE

GHOSTS LIKE IT HOT

DANCES WITH GHOSTS

EXCERPT: SILENCE OF THE GHOST

MURDER BY DESIGN SERIES BOOK #2

"WHY DO I have to be here for this?" I grumbled to Ryan, getting out of my car in the Flats, an area of old warehouses by the Cuyahoga River that had gone through many reinventions and currently had restaurants and loft apartments. "Why can't you two lovebirds look for Hannah's body?"

Immediately I realized that was a horrible sentence. There was nothing romantic about seeking out your own corpse with your equally deceased boyfriend. I felt a flush stain my cheeks, which with my Irish heritage of fair skin and light freckles, was probably highly pronounced. Ryan's eyebrows rose and I made a face. "Sorry, that didn't sound right."

"We can't call the cops if we find something," he reminded me.

He was right. If we found Hannah's body in the last place she remembered being, neither of them could use a cell phone to dial 9-1-1. I was going to have to call the police and explain why I happened to be wandering around the riverbank alone after having spent the earlier part of the day held hostage by a maniacal insurance salesmen. This was going to go over well. I fervently hoped we found nothing but weeds, trash, and mosquitos in the summer heat.

"Fine," I said. "But it's getting late. It's going to be dark soon, and I'm not wandering around here by myself. That's just stupid." It was a muggy, oppressively hot summer day and it smelled like asphalt with a whiff of fried food emanating from one of the nearby restaurants.

Even though I lived one neighborhood over, this was a part of Cleveland I didn't actually frequent that often. I tended to stay in my own area, which had restaurants and bars galore, plus the enormous West Side market. I usually didn't see any reason to fight to find a parking space in this part of town, even though it had great river views. I was probably limiting myself, but I could admit I'd been in something of a rut since Ryan's death. I had stuck to the ease and comfort of being close to home.

Hannah seemed stuck in the car. I gestured to her. "Ryan, I think she needs help figuring out the transport thing you do." Then I glanced around quickly to make sure no one had heard me. I forget sometimes that not everyone sees dead people and a slight redhead in a sundress and wedge sandals talking to herself was a little odd.

"Got it." He popped back into the car then suddenly they

both appeared standing next to me. Ryan eyed my outfit. "You should have changed your shoes."

"I can do anything in heels," I assured him. "And these are wedges, so I'm totally golden."

"I don't know what that means but I'll take your word for it." He scanned the area. "Hannah, where did you and Sam go?"

She pointed toward the bridge. It was a massive iron and steel structure. The pilings were so large they created huge concrete blocks down the side of the embankment. There was some graffiti on a few. In the sun everything shimmered with heat, the weeds still from the lack of a breeze. The river was sluggish, a huge barge equally lazy as it chugged toward Lake Erie.

"We were meeting his dealer."

Her ghostly cheeks actually flushed pink behind her mascara streaks. She didn't meet Ryan's eye.

But he didn't say anything about her falling off the wagon, which I agreed with. It seemed irrelevant at this point if she'd succumbed to her addiction again. What mattered was why she was dead and had appeared in my kitchen. Ryan said it wasn't standard protocol for a ghost to show up so instantaneously, and I believed him, because what did I know about after death details? More than I wanted to, but not enough to understand what the hell was going on.

"So you remember the guy strangling you here? What happened to Sam?"

"He ran," she said. "Before the guy attacked me. He left me there alone with him."

Ryan swore violently. "Asswipe."

Indeed. But then I had an equally horrifying thought. "Wait, how long ago did Hannah die? What if the killer is still here?" I frantically swiveled my head from side to side to make sure no one was creeping up behind me poised to wring my neck. I appeared to be alone, but one would assume killers would be circumspect. This was BS. "I want to go home." There was a bag of Cheetos calling my name.

I had certainly regained an appetite for junk food since Ryan had shown up. It was like I was channeling his cravings. Which was weird.

"Relax. I'll warn you if I see anyone."

"Great, I feel so much better." In order to just get the whole thing over with I started moving through the brush, glancing behind me every two seconds. There was nothing but hard-packed dirt and some stubbly weeds. It had been a dry summer and the brush was withered and brown. It made for an easy job. I could scan everything quickly and move on.

To my right there was a former warehouse that had been turned into apartments, and I could see a man on his small balcony leaning over the railing watching me. I must have looked sketchy as hell and I had no ready explanation for what I was doing. "What do I tell someone if they ask what I'm doing?" I asked Ryan.

"Tell them your phone was stolen from a restaurant and your find my phone app pointed over here."

Oh, good one. "Got it." There was a funky smell mingling with the fried foods and river water. "Gross, what is that nasty stink?"

In hindsight, I blame my cluelessness on being strung out from the day's events and from the two (maybe three) shots of Jameson I had done several hours earlier. But I honestly said, without irony, "Ryan, someone threw a ham down here. Why would someone do that? Geez."

It was rounded chunk of meat, with a reddish-brown leathery coating, like a HoneyBaked ham straight from the store. The front end was rotting, and there were flies crawling all over it. I covered my mouth with my hand to prevent some of the stench from invading my tongue and taste buds. A gag followed. I took it one step further and grabbed my thick auburn hair and covered my nose and mouth.

"Bailey, don't touch it," Ryan said, his voice low and urgent.

"What?" I turned around to make a face. "Why would I do that? That's disgusting."

His expression made me freeze. "That's not a ham, Bai. It's a human thigh."

To read the complete story one-click here: SILENCE OF THE GHOST

About the Author

USA Today and New York Times Bestselling author Erin McCarthy sold her first book in 2002 and has since written over seventy novels and novellas in teen fiction, romance, and mysteries. Erin has a special weakness for tattoos, high-heeled boots, Frank Sinatra, and martinis. She lives with her husband and their blended family of kids and rescue dogs.

Connect with Erin:
www.erinmccarthymysteries.com

Want to know what's next for Bailey in her ghost hunting adventures?
Sign up for release info, contests, and prizes!
Click Here

Made in the USA
Monee, IL
13 August 2020

38238802R00100